D1083342

S

Portrait of a Spy

Portrait of a Spy

RCMP Intelligence – The Inside Story

A novel by IAN ADAMS

GAGE PUBLISHING

All characters in this book are fictional and any resemblance
to persons living or dead is purely coincidental.

ISBN 0-7715-9354-X

Cover Design: Susan Weiss

Printed and bound in Canada by John Deyell Company
1 2 3 4 5   JD   81 80 79 78 77

LIST OF PRINCIPAL CHARACTERS

Superintendent S, former director of
  counter-espionage, B Operations, Security
  Services, RCMP
Inspector DV, an investigator on the Soviet Desk,
  also of B Operations, Security Services, RCMP
Krista Gollner, a government interpreter and S's lover
The SG, the Solicitor General, Cabinet Minister
  responsible for the RCMP
The EA, the Solicitor General's executive assistant
Letourneau, former Director General of Intelligence
Hazelton, editor of a right-wing Toronto newspaper
Atkinson, Toronto television journalist and informer
  on the RCMP payroll
The Old Hand, an Ottawa bureaucrat
Kling, an arms dealer and CIA bagman
The Lawyer, S's legal representative

OTHER CHARACTERS

Daniels, a CIA interrogator
Smellie, a former assistant commissioner of the
  RCMP in charge of Security Services
Mrs. Hazelton, wife of the editor
The Old Lefty, Krista Gollner's father
Molonski, S's right-hand man for fifteen years
Wilson, sub-inspector in charge of the Soviet Desk,
  B Operations, Security Services, RCMP
Bardesio, a right-wing terrorist from Uruguay

"In twenty-five years the RCMP Security Services has caught only one illegal—one real spy. Not a hell of a lot to brag about, is it?"

Inspector DV, RCMP Security Services

For L.J.B.

But most of all for D.V. and T.H.

SECTION I

Strange voyage. S sleeps. His body hurtles through space, always toward the setting sun. Below, massive dark clouds tower, rage purple, and storm across the ocean. He dreams. The violence of the motion that surrounds him enters his flesh. His skin trembles. He dreams with his whole body. Images become shards of mirrors, each bearing a distorted reflection of his own life, that force their way through swollen nerve endings; and finally, wrenched by the forces of his flight, are flung out and left to spin, burnt, pale stars against the grey sky.

What are the nightmares of a man who has only outwardly embraced a minor role in his own life? What shapes force their way through the screens a man like S has erected around his consciousness; and who, in the self-imposed isolation of a spy, has contained his emotions and energies within a labyrinth of games within games? Does he dream, like us, of the flesh made fantasy? And do the dreams turn as he turns, on the spit of his own anxieties; on betrayal, on deception, on disillusion?

A voice, clear and immediate in the vivid images it evokes, surfaces through the upper levels of his nightmare.

"This morning, superintendent . . . " the gentle but insistent voice of Daniels softens the sharp edges of the bare CIA interrogation room. Not even a sheet of paper on the desk. Nothing to divert the eye and relax the tensed mind. Just the simple stark shapes made by the black metal desk against the long narrow window with its own blind view of a plain concrete wall. In his peripheral vision, S can see the dark silent bulk of DV who had escorted him down from Ottawa. DV, a little out of his depth, conveys a sense of embarrassment; a middle-aged man suddenly responsible for a senile father arrested for indecent exposure on a crowded street.

"This morning, superintendent, we are going to discuss your relationship with Kim Philby. . . . "

Even in the depths of his dream S has to laugh. As though anyone ever had any kind of relationship with that remote and masked bureaucrat. Not that he couldn't charm and flatter when he wanted to. But that had only been a role for him to slip into. And of course he had worn other masks, all of them too real: the Cambridge grad with the painful stutter; the taciturn "passport officer" servicing the British consulate in Turkey; the calm and efficient SIS liaison officer to the CIA in Washington; and then, the aloof and snobbish British journalist. They all worked so well. Perhaps too well. For were the roles and masks more than the personas of a superspy? Where they, as S had so often asked himself, to hide the desperation of a man sealed in a role history had reduced to absurdity? How could Kim's idealism, and the energy of his Marxism of the thirties, have remained insensible, unchanged by what had happened to the revolution?

2

Even in S's dreams, thoughts of Philby turned to Gouzenko. But this time the plates of reality and fantasy, slipping and sliding across each other, would not let him focus on the Russian who . . . . Instead, he and Kim are standing on the balcony of a restaurant in Fatih, part of the Old City of Istanbul. Through the glass doors leading to the bar comes the warm and noisy murmur of their colleagues from the British Consulate-General. Kim and S have finished their conversation and in the silence that lies between them, both seem to listen for some secret answer to come from the incomprehensible Turkish voices that drift up to them from the street below. The black night air is moist. It echoes with the haunting sounds of ships leaving the harbor. Wreaths of mist, discolored by gaudy lights, float through the streets.

Ah . . . he had been so happy there. So young. Soft heavy thighs of Armenian women roll voluptuously through his dreams. Life then had been full of mystery: Afternoons of oblique conversations with Greek communist students in crowded coffee houses. Evenings in dim shrouded rooms, heavily scented with tamarind. Small carved wooden tables, inlaid with ivory and carefully positioned on intricately tiled floors. Invariably he would find her in one of the inner rooms. Her name? Was it . . . Aleayh? The gown she always wore, shot silk the color of pale rosewater. It seemed to illuminate the dark corner of her windowless alcove. Her skin always smelled vaguely of oranges. Her tongue, thick, dark red against the glint of gold fillings, coiled in ancient caress. He had been deeply moved to realize how glad she always was to see him. But how real had that been? And when she arched her neck, and

3

her eyelids softly fluttered; when she turned her head aside on the pillow and with a long, gentle groan deeply expelled her breath and filled the air with the fragrance of sen-sen and sweet coffee . . . had that been real? It had seemed so then.

"This morning, Superintendent S, this morning we are going to talk about Sgt. Blake and the payoff made to him in the Glebe supermarket. . . ."

The soft voice of Daniels is somehow swept away by an enlarged bloated hand; his own? It moves downward with horrifying slowness toward the note left on his desk. Does he see it with his own eyes or through the lens of the hidden TV camera they have mounted in the ceiling? The note is from Krista. He had never realized until the day she left that beyond her own narcissism she had a poetic mind. She confessed that she had found it too painful to endure his other women, that she had to leave, even if it brought her more pain. And if it did, well, then she would walk beside the Rideau Canal during Ottawa's soft summer evenings and remember his arm around her waist and the sensation of her long, white cotton dress fluttering around her ankles. Just thinking about that, she wrote, would always make her feel better.

* * * * *

S awoke. We can imagine that he was uncomfortable, his clothes gritty against his skin. His mind, after a fourteen-hour jet flight, a vista of bleak spaces. The plane banked in a long graceful arc over the Sydney suburbs. September in Australia. Spring showers had covered the city with a green translucent wash. Sunlit reflections from hundreds of backyard swimming pools speckled the cityscape which, even at this height, seemed verdant, relaxed and, most of all, inviting.

Sydney, last haven for those Anglophones driven to abandon the past. It holds no promise of a new start, only the security of isolation. The guarantees of the good life, frozen in time. There are no demands that evil be exorcized, that moral flab be flayed. Violence and outrage lie as calm as stagnant ponds in a summer garden. And they all come here: big-time bank robbers; British politicians, cracked, undone by power or the lack of it, arrive on borrowed passports, and with their vapid clinging mistresses, seaweed encountered on the final voyage of a life diverted by minor personality defects; American corporation presidents, surprised in a cash-flow squeeze, descend at Kingsford Smith International Airport, their bewigged and strident personal secretaries on one arm and a bag of US dollars under the other. And why not? The city is somnolent, pleasant, modern in the most western and banal sense of the word. There is no febrile energy of confrontation here to disconcert the newcomer, no curiosity. The citizens are too distracted, left enervated by their massive preoccupation with gambling, sports, and the river of booze that flows through the thousands of pubs and workingmen's clubs. The Australian residence laws — as long as you are white, English-speaking, and have the money — are not impossible to overcome.

S was impatient to escape the plane. The long flight had intensified his always latent claustrophobia. The pressure of his asthma stifled his chest: "Three, four,

5

five,'' he counted, an attempt to find the rhythm that would smooth the chaos of his breathing. His anxiety was heightened by the restless tension given off by the other passengers. They had been on the ground ten minutes. The plane's engines were shut down; the air conditioning off. The air was unbelievably close, made worse by two Australian health officers who, in an odd attempt at preventative medicine, sprayed the cabin with a heavy aerosol disinfectant. The passengers gasped, clapping their hands over their nostrils and mouths.

At last, escape. The air outside the plane was light, full of seductive warmth. Almost immediately the pressure in his chest began to subside. S moved unseeing, unhearing, with the crowd as it straggled wearily toward the immigration and passport control barriers.

Suddenly, a short stocky man blocked his path. A fair bland face, sandy moustache, pale blue eyes, bristly eyebrows. ''Superintendent, I wonder if you would be good enough to come with me for a moment. This way please.'' And even before he had finished speaking, the man placed a hand gently on S's elbow to guide him toward an unmarked door off the hall. A moment later, they were in a small windowless room. DV was there, his large quiet bulk crowding the room. They did not greet each other. S was exhausted, obviously off balance, and presumably caught only a few key words in the short statement DV read to him. Something about ''the Solicitor General . . . special inquiry . . . in camera . . . return on the next plane . . .''

DV: ''I'm not sure he really understood what I was telling him. I remember he asked, 'Do I at least get a chance to sleep over?' ''

6

It was the first time that DV had heard S sound remotely plaintive. The Au. can easily imagine that DV was barely able to keep the hard delighted edge of triumph out of his voice: "I told him the flight left in forty-five minutes, that he could sleep on the plane."

* * * * *

It is time to give you more information about S. (But first the Au. would like to clarify the obvious claims he has made to a certain knowledge of the more intimate areas of S's life. The ability to write sympathetically and coherently not only about a person's dreams but even about his private despair can only come from many hours spent *listening* to another life. For most of us, preoccupied with the energy of our own existence, such a process is a denigration of one's own ego. But for the Au., who after all lives in other people's lives, it is a *déformation professionnel:* You select the target. You listen to that person's friends, enemies, lovers, acquaintances, and slowly a life begins to emerge before you. Sometimes a life contradictory in its aims, rich in emotion and detail, or self-destructive in motive, but always — that is, if you have chosen carefully — fascinating. And the Au. admits to a weakness for the process. For him it carries an excitement and fascination similar to watching the image on an exposed piece of photographic paper slowly evolve under the gentle back-and-forth wash of the developer fluid. The Au. has to confess that for him the process has also become a way of life. He can be found two or three afternoons of any week: a rumpled, middle-aged man seated in a quiet bar or restaurant — in almost any city that he happens to find himself — intently listening to the flow of words that articulate yet another essence. With practice he has learned to discipline his body: to keep it relaxed, passive, an invitation to confession. He has developed small techniques: The speaker's attention can be distracted from the author's eyes — lest they betray too intense an interest — by toying casually with the stem of a glass of red wine. The questions are put softly, gently. Not really as questions. More as linkages, segues of time and context; verbal nudges to loosen the flood of stored images in the speaker's experience. But always the Au. listens, and quietly watches the man or woman opposite him fight and gradually lose the inhibition against telling all. It serves as his own special reward — and revenge. If you asked the Au. what he meant by that, he could only say that it found resonance in a reply he had received when he once asked a friend and once-famous runner why he still continued to run marathons: "Because it releases me from the dread of my own life.")

But let us begin with the information about S that is described as *hard* in RCMP intelligence reports, and *substantive* in the thousands of files kept on Canadian citizens by the Department of the Solicitor General. Superintendent S *Physical characteristics:* fifty-six years of age. Five feet eleven inches. One hundred sixty-eight pounds. *Personal information:* A lifelong bachelor, with no known living relatives. (Au: He has always been careful to hide the heavily sensual dimension of his personality. Consequently, all but a few people mistakenly consider him asexual.) He appears to be in generally good health despite a lifelong asthmatic condition; the cause, stress or allergy, has never been properly diagnosed. His reputation for hard work and his ability to concentrate over long periods of time are legendary. *Profession:* Intelligence.

For all his working life, S has been an officer of that secret world. At the age of forty he was appointed deputy director of counter-espionage of the Security Services of the RCMP. At the age of forty-five, he became the first civilian to be made director of counter-espionage — that is, Superintendent of B Operations — and remained in that post until recently, *i.e.,* for approximately the last ten years.

The Au. wants you to have the beginnings of this profile of Superintendent S so that you will have a more concrete image to hold on to as we weave our way into the central mystery of this story: Why was S, after months of interrogation by, first, his RCMP superiors in Security Services, then by counter-espionage in the Central Intelligence Agency headquarters in Langley, Virginia, and last, by Britain's MI6 (you will note the precise colonial pecking order of the investigation), finally allowed to resign from his job and take an early retirement (age fifty-five, on full pension of $15,000 a year). And then, as we have introduced him, allowed to wing his way to some illusive freedom across the ocean, and presumably out of the reach of Canadian history, only to be arrested, or rather "asked to return" to Canada. Why?

You are warned that at this stage much of the information about S must of course be considered "preliminary" — to use SS jargon. And although the Au. has already spent many hours attempting to verify the information, in interviews with men and women who had known S for fifteen or twenty years, it has become apparent that few *really* knew him. Of course, it often happens that way, doesn't it? People think back and only afterwards realize they have been allowed to *assume* much of what they knew about a person. The people who knew S only reflected the image that he had manufactured for them: his working personality, anecdotes from his youth, reminiscences from his childhood. Here then are the initial quotes and scraps of information — the reflections from the image — that the Au. has so far been able to collect and piece together: There is nothing upper-class about S. Nothing in his birth or background that would put him in that British and privileged old boy's network that launched the careers of Philby and the other Cambridge communists of the thirties.

Instead, his origins are humble, oppressive and lower-middle-class. His mother widowed — when S was four — and an older aunt who dominated his mother; two fussy, rather boring women with few emotional resources to raise a child. Their only source of income was the rooms they rented in their cavernous Victorian house at Southend-on-Sea ("five minutes to the beach," the tiny classified ad always ended) in a scruffy area of that English resort town.

It is no surprise then that S has little nostalgia for his childhood. He remembers ("but only after he had thought about it") long weary hours of enforced idleness. Sunday afternoons, for example, when he yearned to play soccer on the street with friends, kicking about an old ball, were instead spent in the stuffy front parlor with his mother while she "did the books," her weekly ritual, and the only use he can remember the front parlor ever being put to.

He also remembers that he found it easiest to pretend

that he didn't understand what his mother was talking about when she referred to his aunt's occasional liaisons with the odd nondescript lodger. That way he did not have to endure for more than a few minutes his mother's clucks of disapproval and vague moralizing: "Your aunt and I are two completely different people. Always have been, always will," stated in a nasal whine over the noise of pots and pans petulantly banged around on the kitchen stove. And offered, one supposes, to counter any possible stain of what his mother obviously considered to be the doubtful moral example set for him.

But he remembers it was always his aunt who collected the rent in advance and who possessed an unerring eye for the secret drinkers, the deadbeats, and the occasional frowzy prostitute who, client in tow, mistakenly sought a room for a couple of hours. "This is a respectable house, I'll have you know," followed by the door slam that only the true petit bourgeois landlady can time to sound indignant.

Apparently S claims to remember little else about his childhood. (From the CIA and RCMP interrogations DV reports that S was defensive about these gaps in what was usually considered to be a phenomenal ability to memorize and recall detail.) "It was the thirties, the depression years, and for most children of my age and class in Britain it was a desolate and monotonous childhood." He was apparently interested in schoolwork, in which he did well, winning several scholarships. He had just finished grammar school when the Second World War broke out. "Army wouldn't take me; damned asthma, had it all my life. God knows how these things happen, but suddenly

11

found myself with a flunkie's job in the War Department. Turned out to be the cipher division. Took to it all very easily, really. I was looked upon, quite unrealistically I'm afraid, as some sort of prodigy. Finally ended up in a branch that was absorbed by the SIS. And I know what you are going to ask me, everybody always does, (this to the CIA interrogator Daniels) is that when I first met Philby? No, it was much later. After the war, Istanbul, forty-six, forty-seven. Yes. Things were quite hot then. Lots of chaps running around trying to pull the carpet out from under the Greek communists. Succeeded, too, I would say."

"What was Philby like? Well, I really can't say. Didn't have more than a couple of conversations with him. He was quite a standoffish type, you know. And I was very much his junior. At least, he certainly made me feel it."

* * * * *

The problem of dealing with the created image of S became much more complicated for the RCMP officers who were first given the secret and difficult responsibility for investigating S. They were not simply investigating S as a person. They had wanted to measure the effect of his role as director of counter-espionage. How effective had he been in blocking off attempts by hostile agents to insert themselves into the structure of power? How significant was the information-gathering apparatus he had created? But then, you see, S himself, if not always initially responsible for the gathering of that already mentioned *hard* and *substantive* information, the "meat and potatoes" of the Solicitor

General's department, was in the position, indeed charged with the responsibility for processing that same intelligence information upon which the Solicitor General operated. In other words, all counter-espionage, investigative and operational information, flowed through S. Because he had, as we shall see, created over the years a structure that made him a "citizen above suspicion." In other words: NOBODY COULD BEGIN AN INVESTIGATION OF S WITHOUT HIS KNOWING ABOUT IT.

This should give you the first glimpse of the blurred reality, the primary dislocation of focus through which those politicians, bureaucrats, and even some newspaper editors, who believe themselves to be responsible for the security of the state, are forced to regard the real world. And when you relate that displacement of vision to the demands of political expediency, then you have what Sgt. J. Molonski, S's right-hand man for fifteen years, would describe as "bullshit." Unfortunately Sgt. Molonski, a methodical and conscientious policeman, who as a young man believed he had successfully escaped from the farming community of Moosomin in the province of Saskatchewan, had two blind spots: The first was S; the second was that he never understood how dangerous bullshit is for the rest of us.

SECTION II

When the Canadian Pacific Airlines 747 left Fiji for Vancouver, it was almost empty of passengers but still filled with the smell of beer and tobacco, detritus of the noisy vacation-bound Australians who, reinforced by a couple of Sydney soccer teams on a tour of the islands, had flocked off the plane at Nandi.

In this exhausted after-the-party atmosphere, DV watched S wearily fold the armrests out of the way and then lie down across a line of seats. A tall fair-haired and sun-bronzed steward spread a blanket over S and offered him another pillow. Wordlessly, S accepted these attentions. Ever since their encounter at Sydney airport, S had withdrawn into a state of silence and tension that DV had not seen before in his former chief. DV now gazed, not without sympathy, at the middle-aged man, some ten years his senior, who lay stretched out on the seats across the aisle. It struck DV that neither the fatigue that bloated S's face nor the dimmed light of the cabin could entirely hide the intelligence and discipline of his features.

For the last five years, DV had pursued S from the shadows. It had been a marathon. Most of the time he had felt like the runner who always ran on the leader's shoulder, let the leader set the pace, the strategy. DV would simply stay with him to savor the psychological reward that comes to a man when he perceives that he cannot be shaken off. He had been outranked, obstructed by senior and politically more ambitious officers in Security Services, but DV had held on, obsessed with S to the point that his pursuit — as we shall see — became disastrous to his career and his personal life. Perhaps his saving grace, the tenuous handhold that kept him from tumbling down the dark face of his own life, was that he never came to believe that he was more intelligent than S, that he could ever personally outwit or trap S. Over the years he had become too impressed by S's intellect and personal discipline to ever do that. "It kept me humble and it kept me sane," he would later tell the Au. "Try to imagine the level of commitment, the incredible will and discipline required for S to live like that year after year. It is almost incomprehensible . . ." and his voice trailed off. No, DV had only sought to wear S down, to run him to ground, and then let the other, more powerful forces of the hunt take over.

"I was," DV said, "still in awe of him. I remember that I looked at him stretched out in the plane like that and thought, 'Well, Superintendent S, this time we've got you,' when he suddenly sat up and leaned across the aisle to demand: 'Inspector, do you really think that I went to Australia to wait it out? To wait for *them* to let me come in?'

"No, he wasn't angry, it was more . . . shall we say, derisive. He sounded so confident." S, it seems, could just as well have been back in his padded green chair in his office at Alta Vista Drive, at the peak of his power as director of counter-espionage, gently mocking some underling who thought that he had come up with a brilliant analysis of the secret game as it was being played out in some corner of Ottawa.

"It really shook me up. I simply stared back into his face." Then, even more astonishing, S became a man DV had never seen before. "Sergeant," he sneered, conveniently forgetting, or implying that DV should never have been commissioned, and using the rank the way it is always used to needle NCOs in Security Services, "this is *not* Beirut, this is *not* 1961, I am *not* Kim Philby. The truth, Sergeant, is that Canadian intelligence after all these years is still playing catch-up."

"You should know, sir," DV replied, "after all, you have been leading Canadian intelligence all these years." S then turned away with a gesture of disgust, lay down and closed his eyes.

"I admit it wasn't one of your wittiest replies, but for a moment I was shaken. At first his confidence was incredible. And all the old doubts welled up in me. But you know, in that moment of abrupt shift in mood, I sensed something had changed inside him. Underneath that hard sneer there was, well not exactly desperation. I don't really know how to describe it except that . . . to be truthful it reminded me of the old days, when I worked as a narcotics detective and had a suspect against an alley wall and threatened to beat the piss out of him. . . S's body gave off this strange smell. His breath was sour, fetid. You know the old cliché about the cornered animal turns to fight? Perhaps there was an element of that to it . . ."

The rest of the flight was uneventful, S silent, con-

DV had not expected anyone to show up at the airport, and shrugged, "I thought perhaps it was some commanding officer's warped sense of humor that had sent Molonski down to greet his former boss." Molonski did not acknowledge S, and S remained quiet. He must have sensed that there had been a sudden change of plan that made DV uneasy. Molonski and DV flashed their identification to get through customs and immigration, but when they arrived at the departure section, there were a few minutes when DV had to leave Molonski and S while he checked through their tickets to Ottawa. "I took only two or three minutes, but when I looked around they had gone. I tried to think how far they could have moved in that short a space of time. And I'll tell you the back of my neck was icy cold." DV became aware of several doors. Two led to the men's and women's washrooms. In between was a third. On the front it had a jagged symbol of electrical power and a DANGER — KEEP OUT sign printed in large letters. "It had to be the one. I was in there like a shot. Molonski had S pinned against the wall of this tiny room jammed with electrical equipment, his hands — they're just like meat hooks — wrapped around S's throat. As soon as I closed the door behind me, Molonski let go, and S just folded to the floor like a bundle of rags. I ignored Molonski — the last thing I wanted to do was tangle with that brute — and went to work on S. He was gasping for air and I could hear his lungs wheezing and banging away. But, I'll tell you, he looked really happy to see me. Molonski? He took off. In no great hurry. As he went out the door, he turned back: 'Try and take better care of him, he has a serious asthma condition.' Then he nodded to S on the floor. 'Enjoyed our little chat.' Just like that, very cool, then he left."

After S was able to get to his feet, DV made some telephone calls — "not from the RCMP airport office." Half-an-hour later they were surrounded by a group of men and led to a Canadian Armed Forces plane that flew them to Ottawa. But it was a long half-hour wait for his military escort, and DV made S go with him to the washroom so he could take his .38 out of his briefcase and put on his shoulder holster. "When I look back, I suppose it seems incredibly naive, given that I am supposed to be an intelligence officer, but I assumed that everybody was going to play this one out as an intellectual exercise. But suddenly it had come to me that there were a lot of people who would like to see S dead."

* * * * *

DV is an impressive man. Not that tall, just over six feet. But with an enormous breadth of shoulders and powerful chest. (In his youth he was a popular and successful athlete; for two years in a row the Ontario provincial Greco-Roman wrestling champion.) His face is usually without expression, except that he has the watchful eyes of a street-wise cop. (Au: Which he is, narcotics for two years, before intelligence. "Okay," they said, "now forget you were ever a cop. Here, in Intelligence, we don't make busts.") It is ironic that he marvels so continually at S's sanguine manner for DV seems totally confident of himself physically, and further, has the air of a man who knows exactly what he is doing now, and what he will do next.

For a self-educated man, DV is surprisingly well-read. Certainly an expert on everything that has been written on his own profession. And along the way, he has developed an interesting appreciation of Trotsky, at least from a policeman's perspective. Reading about Dzerzhinsky, 'the Savanarola of the Revolution', Lenin's and the Soviet Union's first security chief, led him to Trotsky. It was Dzerzhinsky who complained at the time of Lenin's death: "Only saints or scoundrels can serve in the GPU, but now the saints are running away — and I am left with the scoundrels." (DV: "An inevitable problem, it seems, of intelligence organizations.") Obviously fascinated by the quirks of fate around which history turns, DV disguises his interest with irreverence: "I often wonder what would have happened if Trotsky hadn't been seriously ill when Lenin died; if he hadn't had to spend two months on the Black Sea coast to recuperate. By the time he got back, it was too late, wasn't it? Stalin had the polit-bureau sewn up and Trotsky by the nuts."

At the age of forty-two DV's failures are his job and his marriage. As an investigator on the Soviet desk, he is stuck, passed over too many times to really hope for a substantial promotion. It was only after eighteen years, nine of them as a sergeant, that he was finally given a commission and made an inspector. But it was done almost as an afterthought. Although it was generally acknowledged among those "in the know" at headquarters that it was done to keep him around — nobody knew more about the "operational history" of the force, as it was rather patronizingly put. (There was a bit more to it than that: DV had often covered up for a fellow officer, or, with his intimate knowledge of

20

the force's inner workings, helped salvage at least the *appearance* of an otherwise disastrous operation, and thus saved the responsible officer from further damage in those mysterious and often bizarre struggles that go on from time to time within the Security Services. He had, in other words, "many debts owed him.")

But there is more wistfulness than bitterness in his tone when he talks about his work. "I was always too busy running the store. The bright young guys were sent to university and got the promotions. And then I'm always making trouble for myself with management. We have no union, you know. Always thought that unfortunate," an ironic comment made with a wry grin.

DV won't talk about his marriage. He lives alone in a sparsely furnished one-bedroom apartment in an Ottawa highrise. In the bedroom, one plain double bed; in the living room, one ancient but comfortable leather armchair, "The sole material object to survive my marriage"; along one wall a crowded clutter of books, files, and magazines that have long since spilled over the makeshift brick-and-board extension to the original bookcase. In the dining area, a formica kitchen table with two plastic upholstered chairs, all worn. At one end of the table, the end which receives the light from the glass balcony doors, a small brown Olympia portable typewriter with a piece of lined paper rolled into the platten. (After several visits over a six-month period, the Au. became convinced that it was always the same piece of paper.) On a hook on the bathroom door, a worn and stained track suit. A grey T-shirt with the words "REVOLUTION IS THE OPIATE OF THE INTELLECTUALS" printed on the front. (A present from his son.) And on the floor behind the door, a battered pair of size ten-and-a-half Nike running shoes. On the kitchen window sill, a stunted plant that a woman friend had given DV, but which he had obviously forgotten to water sufficiently. In all, an image of a preoccupied bachelor, wary of the physical decline of middle age, and probably spending too much time alone.

From other sources the Au has learned that DV has a teenage son, already a remarkable athlete, with a promising career, if he wants it, as a professional hockey player. About DV's wife: There is at this time very little information except that she is intelligent, independent, and has her own career as a fairly highly placed bureaucrat in the Ministry of Supply and Services. The only vaguely objectionable characteristic about her is a sometimes venemous breath. No doubt, the informant reports, as a consequence of her obsession with low-carbohydrate diets. "It's the ketones," the informant, a biochemist, added somewhat apologetically and perhaps in response to a raised eyebrow. "In the absence of carbohydrates one's metabolism burns accumulated body fat. The ketones, really carbon fragments of the process, are excreted and also expelled in the carbon dioxide one breathes out. That's the physiological process. In reality, it becomes a gas with a rather penetrating odor."

* * * * *

To paint in at this point what might at first seem to be a digression, but in fact is invaluable and fascinating background, it is necessary that the Au. take the reader

22

back in time a few months (to be precise, June 12) before S's interrupted visit to Australia — a rather abrupt departure, following the RCMP "request to return" to Canada for the in-camera hearings that have been demanded by the Solicitor General.

It is just after two; an afternoon of brilliant spring sunshine in the sprawling western suburbs of Toronto. A short plump man waits at a bus stop on the west side of Royal York Rd. Behind him is a wasteland of concrete and asphalt, an anonymous cityscape of cheaply built highrise apartments. These are the "stacked dormitories for the factory workers of the western sector of the city," a phrase used by the *Toronto Star*, the city's largest newspaper. Constructed by one of the three or four developers that dominate construction in the city, they are designed to accommodate, at exorbitant prices the city's new immigrant population. The apartments are sold as condominiums with low down payments and staggering interest rates — so as to give the new arrivals at least the impression, however fleeting, of the benefits of ownership.

There is no focal point or sense of community to these suburbs; only the occasional small ugly shopping plaza breaks the monotony of concrete highrises. It is also a "get lost district," another *Star* phrase, for those illegal workers from Europe and Latin America who hold no legal work or residence permits.

The man who stands at the bus stop is Latin American — Uruguayan — and his heavy dark face carries the evidence of Indian blood. His name is Nelson Marzos Bardesio. The fear that is obvious in that fat and bloated face, which earned him the nickname of

"The Frog" in his native city of Montevideo, is entirely understandable. Because across the street, two men in a rented Plymouth are openly watching Bardesio. Worse, the passenger in the back seat is busy photographing Bardesio with a telephoto lens. It is the second time that day he has seen them. The first time was when he came off the night shift at a nearby plant where he works as a security guard.

The last time in his life strange men in large cars showed unusual interest in Bardesio was February 24, 1972. For Bardesio it was the beginning of a long slow slide into despair. The men were Tupamaros, left-wing urban guerrillas of Montevideo. They "arrested" Bardesio and held him in a "people's prison" for eighty-six days. The Tupamaros considered themselves the "conscience of Uruguay"; from the beginning of their movement in 1968 they spent their energies on exposure of corruption in big business, government and the military forces. There was a quixotic elan to their operations, carried out with brilliance and daring, that no doubt was the reason they captured the imagination of the public with such unprecedented rapidity. And which, in turn, no doubt accounts for the brutality and torture with which they have since been put down by the succeeding military dictatorships of Uruguay.

The Tupamaros pride themselves on information, on the accuracy and quality of information they present to the population. Before his capture, Bardesio had been identified by the Tupas as a photographer and intelligence officer of the Uruguayan secret police, *Direccion de Intelligencia y Informacion*. But his role was much more than that; for Bardesio was the right-hand man to William Cantrell, a CIA agent posing as a

United States AID officer, who in fact was directing the Montevideo police force in counter-insurgency operations against the Tupamaros.

With their ironic brand of gallows humor, Latin American leftists have dubbed Cantrell "the father of electricity" — in recognition of the role he has played in introducing and training Latin American police forces in the use and technique of torture by electric shock.

Senora Silva Araujo Roggerone, age 30, was arrested as she walked to work. She was taken to police headquarters and there stripped and beaten by two police officers who kept demanding where the arms were hidden. As Senora Roggerone knew nothing she could not tell them anything. She was hung upside down with her knees draped over what is called the Parrot's Perch, a metal bar, two metres off the floor. Her body was hosed down with water so as to allow the electricity to pass more efficiently over her skin. Electrical leads from a high-voltage transformer, housed in a large black suitcase — the voltage of which can be regulated by the interrogator — were attached by means of alligator clips to those parts of her body where the nerve endings are particularly sensitive: her ear lobes, nostrils, mouth, nipples, vagina, and anus. When the police interrogator switched on the current, "the pain," testified Senora Roggerone, "came in endless waves. It threw my body into uncontrollable convulsions. I was tortured for over a period of 48 hours. I could not bear it. I pleaded with them to kill me." Senora Roggerone signed a confession that she had led the police to a hidden arms cache. In court all police charges against her were dropped; it was apparently a case of mistaken identity. Senora Roggerone is confined to a wheelchair for the rest of her life. (From the reports of Amnesty International, Jan. 1977)

Bardesio was well treated by the Tupamaros. They even engineered a "visit" to the People's Prison by the president of the Chamber of Deputies, (Au: equivalent to the Speaker of the House of Commons) Hector Gutierrez Ruiz. The information obtained from this visit by Senor Ruiz was used by a Uruguayan senator, Enriques Erro as a document of evidence read into the Senate record.

In this document Bardesio confessed that he had been a member of a Death Squadron organized by Cantrell and other CIA agents. That he himself had participated in the bombings of houses in which lived not necessarily leftist, but liberal, doctors, journalists, and other opponents of the military-supported regime. He also confessed that he had participated in the torture and murder of two leftists, one, Hector Castagnetto da Rosa, a student leader.

Bardesio's confessions were the first real hard evidence of the CIA-organized death squads in Latin America, and they created an enormous furor among the population. Bardesio was finally released by the Tupamaros into the custody of two judges who obtained safe-conduct guarantees for him from the military authorities.

The CIA did not want Bardesio around for any legal

investigations and so they whisked him out of the country to Canada where, in one of those accommodating "middle-management deals" that are made between secret services, he was allowed by the RCMP to take up residence in Toronto. (DV: "Why not, we're supposed to be the cultural and economic dumping ground for the US so what difference does an agent here or there make? Besides, Canada is an ideal place to 'ice' FBI or CIA agents and informers until they can return to their home ground without fear of reprisal.")

Bardesio's problem was that he didn't stay "on ice." Impatient with his job as a night security guard, he sought out intelligence officers on Toronto police forces, and offered his services as an informer in the Latin American community. This effort at upward mobility became known to some Tupamaros who had themselves sought refuge in Toronto. They have warned Bardesio that they will kill him if he continues to betray his own people in a foreign country. And that is why Bardesio is now standing in the warm June sunshine, shivering with fear.

But this time Bardesio is safe. The two men are only journalists, and Bardesio is able to catch the next bus unharmed. The next week a left-wing journal carries the story of Bardesio in Toronto and a report of his police activities in Uruguay. It takes several weeks for the established press to react to the story. During that time, an opposition NDP member queries the minister of immigration who, in turn, queries the Solicitor General — the minister responsible for the RCMP. The Solicitor General, sensing a possible scandal, orders the RCMP to get Bardesio out of the country. Bardesio disappears, and at last report is understood to be taking "religious training" in Mexico City.

* * * * *

Ordinarily the Solicitor General — the SG — does not tell the RCMP what to do. The RCMP runs itself, and any politician who wants to survive learns to leave the RCMP alone. That is why the Minister's portfolio also contains responsibility for the federal prison system — it gives the minister something to do. Which may account in some way for the phenomenon that proportionately Canada puts more people behind bars than any other country in what is known as "the western democratic industrialized world", or "the developed countries of the free world", or "advanced western societies" (Au: take your pick).

In any event, the SG is not widely respected for his rational behaviour; as we shall see, he is, in fact, "his own worst enemy. And if it wasn't that Canada's government and its workings are continually shrouded in such paranoid secrecy, the minister would have long ago been revealed and thrown out of office for being the crass and corrupt bumbler that he is." This from the SG's executive assistant, an otherwise well-spoken young man educated in the Liberal elitist tradition (Upper Canada College; Université de Montreal, M.A., political history; Osgoode Hall, Bachelor of Laws.) He does not attempt to hide his contempt for the minister. "Every time he shits he has a brain hemorrhage." The same well-educated and well-spoken EA knows that the SG's survival is based on two quali-

28

ties: First, his unswerving loyalty to the Prime Minister, "There is no political dirty work or butchery, no matter how unprincipled, that he will not carry out if called upon to do so by the PM." Second, his intimate and detailed knowledge of the political patronage system that keeps the Prime Minister's party in power. It was after all the political proving ground through which the SG, a lawyer, labored and rose to catch the PM's attention. He also believes that he has an ace in the hole. Molonski: "When the Prime Minister came to power, he sent the SG in to get the file the RCMP Security Services had built up on the PM over the years. The PM wanted the file shredded, especially the one on his wife. But before the SG did so, I know that he had his own personal copy made. The guy has the courage and cunning of a shit-house rat."

It would be a mistake for the reader to think of the Solicitor General, hated and feared as the PM's butcher, as a lonely and disliked man. No, he is by nature a gregarious type. He is the "aggressive small man" who can very successfully play the role of "the man's man." And, according to his EA, he has that "certain attractive charm that accompanies the totally unethical character." He is married, with a family, a favorite mistress — installed as a director on the board of a Montreal company that is in reality a front for the CIA in Canada — and funded in part by the Security Services. He also has a handful of minor mistresses dotted through his corridor of political power as it surges, well oiled, back and forth between Ottawa and Montreal. But like all men he *is* vulnerable. His weakness is part of his success, for he has developed an overweening arrogance — the special blindness of the overreacher. The man who forgets he is protected only because his master has good use for him.

* * * * *

"Look, this is the way the Security Service works." DV takes a paper serviette from its metal holder and with a ballpoint pen sketches a quick schematic of the organization of the Security Services. "At the head you have the DGI, Director General of Intelligence. He holds the rank of deputy commissioner, and theoretically he is supposed to go through the Commissioner, but he also has the machinery to go directly to the Solicitor General or even to the Prime Minister who is chairman of the Cabinet Committee on Security.

"Okay? . . . under the DGI there are three assistant commissioners to help him run the Security Service which is basically split down the middle between operational and administration. The side you are interested in is the operational. Right, you still with me? Okay, let's draw a few more little boxes here." (The Au. has reproduced the organizational chart at the back of the book for those who have an interest in such structures.) "Security Services is broken down into roughly nine operations: A is security screening. If you ever want a government job, you have to be cleared by these guys. God help you if you are a homosexual. You'll never make it. And even if you're not, a lot of the time they may cross your name up with somebody who is a homosexual, or perhaps even find a cousin of yours who is. It all depends on who interprets the data on the computer: how insecure he is about his own sex life, or

30

how reactionary his politics are, and so on. Half the time people never get a government job, and they never know why. Usually it's because of some comment made by the guys in A Operation.

"B Operation is counter-espionage, S's old outfit. That's broken into groupings of desks. Most important, the Soviet desk; and then the Soviet Bloc countries, all broken down into desks. Then there is the Cuban desk — that's the one the CIA is always trying to manipulate.

"D is counter-subversion. These guys also have desks. Main targets are the unions and university campuses. Informers in all the major union structures. Infiltrators in every political organization, sometimes two or three in every important organization. Thousands of dollars are paid every week to informers in the unions, and any kind of left or left-ethnic organization is guaranteed to have at least one D Operations informer.

"E is electronic surveillance. A lot of civilians here. Guys who install all the bugs and phone taps — the latter being mostly illegal. Oh, Christ, yes, they'll bug anybody on the least suspicion. How much do their superior officers know? Well, let's put it this way. They cover their ass by not wanting to know too much. I once talked to a CIA guy who had been in Vietnam. I asked him how they explained away all those Vietnamese civilians who were killed. 'Simple,' he said, 'if you were Vietnamese *and* dead you were VC.' It's the same rational in E Operations — if you are suspect *and* bugged, that makes you subversive.

"F is for files. Lots of grimy work goes on here. Because not only is this operation charged with maintaining files, they also have to develop new ones. Yeah, sure, every politician has a file here. They use the services of homosexuals and prostitutes to build up personal information on everyone: high-ranking corporate executives, cabinet ministers, journalists.

"F Operation is one of those institutional monsters that have been created, and, quite frankly, is out of control. Informers are paid, so it follows they're going to produce information so that they can keep on receiving money. If there is no real information they will fabricate some or report rumors. It's a growth industry. In the Security Services, information is currency. It doesn't matter whether it's counterfeit or inflated currency, it legitimizes the work of the officer who is running the informer. In turn, that legitimizes the work of his superior officer, the Branch, the budget, the computers, the data banks. With all that economic and technological freight on the track, nobody is going to ever start questioning the *quality* of the information. It exists — record it. So the information ends up in the data banks. True or false it will be there forever. How do they grade the information? Officially there are three levels. The first is *hard,* substantive and corroborated information. The second is considered firm, but unsubstantiated. The third is basically reported rumor and gossip. But if they really applied these standards, half the files would be empty. What kind of people are on the payroll? Well, as I said, a lot of it's grimy. There are an awful lot of hookers and homosexual prostitutes on the payroll. Remember Gerda? Yes, well, she started out working for the CIA in West Germany, then when she drifted over here the CIA still had her on the payroll and also talked Security Services into putting her on theirs. Then she started partying with some of our cabinet ministers, which didn't become a scandal until five years later when it broke in the House. Remember all that nonsense about reporters tracking her down in Berlin? Hell, I know the guy in the Security Services who tipped off the reporter on where she was living. As I say, pretty grimy stuff. F Branch also works through the old-boy network to develop their files. For example, the security officer of the Chateau Laurier is an ex-RCMP officer. On a recent Saturday night, he phones up the duty officer at F Operations. Tells him a certain cabinet minister has a fifteen-year-old girl in one of the hotel rooms. The duty officer says, 'Thanks very much.' They whistle a couple of buggers from E Operations over there to tape whatever they can from the next room, and then it all goes into the computer tape. And of course it's all coded. No, not the information, just how it's indexed. For example, the PM's code name is Sea Lion.

"And then they have double sets of files. Say a cabinet minister storms in and demands to see his file. They push a button and produce the same innocuous information you would find in *Who's Who*.

"Okay, then we have H. This is the Chinese section. One special section devoted to counter Chinese communist espionage. Personally, I think, and from everything I hear about it, H is a bit of a joke. When we first recognized the People's Republic of China, they tried sending a couple of RCMP officers to learn Cantonese. The result was nothing to rave about. So they went to the only places they could enlist help: Taiwan and Hong Kong. Everybody knows that the group from Taiwan all have to be CIA plants, and then any policeman you get from Hong Kong has got to be a very doubtful package.

"I is the Watcher Service. Physical surveillance teams. S's baby. He created I Operation, fed it and nourished it. People who wanted to join the Force but couldn't make it for a whole variety of reasons: too tall, too short, too old, not enough education, and so on. Great bunch of people. Long history of bad treatment by the cavalry officers. Why? Because they're civilians. Once the watchers clam on to you, they'll never lose you, and you would never know they were there. I'll tell you more about them later.

"J is electronic operations specialists. These guys are too good for the average bugging job that E Operations does. They have a couple of those laser bugging toys they've picked up from the FBI for about $200,000 apiece. What do they use them for? Say they have this Soviet attaché under surveillance. He's sitting in a car in a downtown Ottawa parking lot with all the windows rolled up, talking to a Canadian citizen. You want to know what they're talking about. The guys from J Operation roll up their laser, aim it at one of the windows. The laser beam picks up the voice vibrations on the glass, and converts them into a tape-recorded conversation at the other end of the machine. Cute, eh?

"L Operations are the thugs. These are the guys who are the enforcers and do all the harassment of leftists, or even politicians, the Force has decided to dislike. They're behind all the break-ins that started in the sixties. Bunch of psychos. I know one guy. Gets his jollies by going over to bars in Hull where he provokes fights so that he can kick the shit out of someone. They were originally put together as a counter-terrorist unit for Quebec and were kept together supposedly to deal with airline hijackings. Now they're being absorbed into D Operation. I once got drunk with one of those guys. He claimed he was part of a combined RCMP-military intelligence unit that went over to Paris to kill that FLQ guy who was found murdered in his hotel room, the one that was supposed to come back to Montreal to take over the FLQ. It's possible. These guys are pretty thick with military intelligence. Most of them have been to Northern Ireland as 'observers.' But, as I said, most of the Security Service guys look upon them as wingy thugs and tend to shun them. But look, here's our hot and sour soup.''

* * * * *

Sauce stains, fragments of beef dumplings, orange chicken, and garlic shrimp lie spattered over the white tablecloth. (''If you want to get anything out of DV, if you want to build some rapport, take him to a good Chinese restaurant. It's a weakness he acquired on his Hong Kong tour.'') DV lingers, chopsticks in hand, over the table, reluctant to accept the end of the meal. ''I could eat this every day, I've always thought French cuisine highly overrated. Hong Kong? Most enjoyable two years I ever had on the Force. No, it was just before Letourneau's regime. But some of us had already started to do work he made policy when he became Director General of Security Services.

''Officially we were liaison officers supposed to do visa control work. Check out the backgrounds of would-be immigrants to Canada. Not so easy in a place like Hong Kong, most corrupt police force in the world. Their chief, a Brit, just retired. The income tax people keep asking him: 'How is it, sir, that you have this four million dollars in your piggybank?' So what do you do when a Mr. Chan walks in and says: 'I want to immigrate to Canada and right here is two million cash to start up a plastic sandal factory in Vancouver'? Well, you start with the Hong Kong police and they say, 'Mr. Chan? No, sorry, never heard of him.' Then you go talk to a couple of friendly intelligence officers. You find out that Mr. Chan is quite active as an international arms dealer and that he also has a cute little sideline exporting opium from Thailand. So you can see why it is important to develop a network of contacts with intelligence officers. (Au: Secret agents from western allied capitalist countries always refer to *themselves* as intelligence officers — men and women from socialist and communist countries are spies. The description also has contradictions with interesting racial overtones, e.g. all Latins, even those trained by the CIA, are always called spies.)

"Of course that didn't stop Mr. Chan. He now, by the way, owns a lot of real estate in Vancouver, and a chunk of Yonge St. in Toronto. But I'm not responsible for those decisions. I just made sure the government knew who they were dealing with. Anyway, we don't do much visa control work any more. You see, Letourneau was a pretty sophisticated guy. Long background first in military intelligence, then in external, later made a diplomat. He knew what the score was. He understood very well that places like West Berlin, Beirut, and Hong Kong are the intelligence markets; that there are men and women in those cities who have information to sell. This is one of those worldly facts that an assistant commissioner of the RCMP, who has spent most of his life wrestling with British Columbia's lower mainland traffic problems, might not be exactly sensitive to. So after Letourneau took over, liaison officers spent maybe three hours a week on immigration visas. The rest of the time is now used to develop contacts and information with other intelligence officers. It's a pleasant way to make a living.''

* * * * *

"Why did Letourneau quit after only a couple of years? Who knows? Sure, it certainly surprised a lot of people. My guess is that he woke up one morning and said to himself: 'Life is too short to spend it with these dumb cavalry officers. The commissioner of the Force is only a caretaker and a fool to boot. The Solicitor General is an asshole. There is nothing I can do to change the structure of the Force, and it is obvious that the Prime Minister is afraid to.' So then I suppose he phoned to tell them he wouldn't be in that morning and then rolled over and went back to sleep.

"To answer the question of why the Prime Minister would be afraid to change the structure of the RCMP, you have to go back to 1969: the Royal Commission on National Security. It was all in camera, of course, but it was obvious that the members of the commission were not impressed by the RCMP's intelligence service. The RCMP had done a lousy job on security. Talk to any security officer who has been around for a while. In twenty-five years, the RCMP security service has caught only one illegal, one real spy. He was a dumb KGB agent, supposedly trained as a hit man. His mission was to find Gouzenko and kill him, but he made only a halfhearted attempt to find Gouzenko. And to be frank, we didn't so much catch him on the job as he turned himself in. Hardly an intelligence coup.

"The members of the commission into national security were told about a few other bizarre incidents, nothing to restore their faith, but I'll get to those some other time because I know you want to stay on the track of this Letourneau thing. The Minister of Justice had no great liking for the RCMP. He is from Montreal and thinks the guys there are out of control and is dumb enough to say so publicly. He suggests a *civilian* intelligence agency! Yeah, something like the CIA.

"Well, all hell breaks loose. The RCMP brass are terrified of losing control over their intelligence-gathering role. Because they know that without it they lose any real political power they have. They would be just another bunch of cops — a contract police force. There was also a very real practical problem: Where do you get a lot of trained civilians to suddenly take over the country's intelligence apparatus? They all have to resign from the RCMP first, right? Anyway, the cavalry officers began to tear the place apart. Don't forget that although they haven't done a very good job of catching spies, they know, politically speaking, where all the bodies are buried. They know an awful lot about the indiscretions, personal and otherwise, of most politicians and bureaucrats, and they can apply a lot of pressure at the most sensitive and vulnerable points in the political system's power structure. I'll tell you about some of those, too, later. No, hell, I'll tell you a good one now.

"One of the guys in operations in Montreal planted a bug in the apartment of a cabinet minister's girlfriend. Apparently it's a stormy relationship. She is trying to get him to leave his wife. So anyway, they transfer what they get from the bug to a cassette tape. The minister has the habit of taking the fast train to Ottawa from Montreal. On the way up, he listens to debriefings from his aides on his own cassette tape recorder. Right, you've got the picture. The operations guy who made the switch sits across the aisle. He tells me it was the funniest thing he's seen in his life. The minister calmly plugs the earphone in his ear, punches the button, and the first thing he hears is this harridan of a mistress screaming in his ear: 'Martin, you're nothing but five pounds of shit stuffed into a four-pound bag.' Apparently he almost has a heart attack, turns white, face starts twitching. Rips the plug out of his ear. Gazes around. He is definitely in a state of shock.

"I guess the whole episode proved the minister's argument. That the guys in Montreal *were* out of control, but he understood the point being made because he never continued to press the issue after that. At least, not publicly. Confronted by all this turmoil, the PM gives up and Letourneau becomes the compromise — a civilian with a lot of intelligence experience, grudgingly acceptable to the RCMP brass, becomes the new Director General of Security Services.

"And you know, I've always been convinced S set the reaction in motion. Sure, the RCMP brass didn't want to lose Intelligence to a civilian agency, but you know most of them wouldn't be able to find their way to work in the morning if they didn't have a driver to take them there. It was S who organized that campaign. I'm sure that he sensed his days were numbered. But he wanted to hang on for two or three more years, which is what he achieved. Yes, it's true that S, as director of the counter-espionage section, would be junior and answerable to Letourneau, but power is rarely exerted through the strict lines of an organizational chart. S had been there since day one. He had all the cavalry officers on his side, completely convinced of the good job he was doing. More, over the years they had promoted him to his present position. For years he had made them look good with his slick reports. All their self-worth, their self-recognition, was invested in S. There is no doubt that he could have generated a lot of resistance to Letourneau's policies, no matter how brilliant they may have appeared. You have to admire S, he really knew how to play both ends against the middle.

"Look, just say Letourneau already knew what S was all about. And it is quite possible that he might have. Don't forget Letourneau has wartime intelligence contacts that go back to Britain's SIS, and of course with the CIA guys who have spent years trying to uncover the KGB network that sustained Philby, Burgess, and Maclean when they worked here in North America. They were intelligence officers obsessed with the hunt for the legendary 'Fourth Man'. Say he knew these guys and they had given him a lot of interesting stuff on S, but in the end nothing he can really use because it couldn't be proved.

"And so, instead, he decides to move against S for the simple straightforward reason of incompetence — one spy in twenty-five years is not a hell of a lot to brag

40

about, is it? — well, he couldn't even do that. Because again the senior members of the Force would be made to look ridiculous wouldn't they? It would lay them open to the question of why they had protected and promoted an incompetent over all those years to the level of director of counter-espionage. To reveal one highly placed government official's lifelong work as meaningless is difficult enough in itself. To expose a whole group of highly placed and powerful men for the same reason is impossible. At least, not without some kind of revolution.''

DV's tone has become a strange mixture of anger and cynical laughter. He begins to speak again, but some inner switch is thrown and, in an unpredictable change of mood and action that the Au. has come to recognize as part of his personality, insists they leave the restaurant immediately. ''Let's walk this food off,'' he says, rising to his feet. ''At our age we can't afford to get any fatter by sitting around talking too much.''

* * * * *

DV is a good walker. And as in all his physical activity, he seems to be able to gracefully pace his stride to the rhythms of speech. And so when he speaks about S as he strolls along Rideau Street, it is without effort or a break in concentration. The Au. gets the feeling that DV is not really talking to him directly but has really integrated the Au. as a supporting actor, a witness to DV's obsession. The Au., not entirely unaware of his therapeutic role, and with his own interests in mind, is content to let DV lead.

''S arrived in Canada in 1952. I would have to check

41

a file to be precise about the month. Again, I'm not sure whether he came directly from the UK or from Hong Kong where he had been working for MI6. Frankly, I don't keep the details of his beginnings in my head. Perhaps that's a function of age. One tends to become more preoccupied with how things end rather than how they start. He was given a minor research-cum-administrative job at Special Branch, as it was then called, at RCMP headquarters in Ottawa, A Division.

"At the time of S's arrival, the art of counter-espionage in Canada was primitive, to say the least, and there was a strong tendency — in true colonial fashion — on the part of headquarters people in Ottawa to look at the British as the model on which they would pattern themselves. This was, of course, all before Philby jumped ship and the British were still exploiting the mystique they had created for themselves as super intelligence officers during the war. The CIA was about to find out the hard way — primarily through the Philby affair — the reality behind some of the myths.

"Much of the RCMP's lack of confidence was also founded on our mismanagement of the Gouzenko affair in 1945. If the force had been in any way prepared, had any intelligence apparatus to speak of, we would have known that Gouzenko was ready to defect, to escape from the Soviet Embassy in Ottawa. He should not have had to run around Ottawa pleading with newspaper reporters to listen to him. If we had been prepared, we would have said, 'Okay, you'll get Canadian citizenship and a lifelong pension, but first you have to go back in there to your cipher job in the Soviet

Embassy and start pumping the information out to us: codes, KGB and GRU staff, Canadian contacts, and so on.' But of course it didn't happen that way. In fact Mackenzie King wanted to feed Gouzenko back to the Soviets . . . Can you imagine? What probably saved Gouzenko's life was that the guy they called Intrepid (Au: code name for Bill Stephenson, MI6 chief in Washington) happened to be in Ottawa, found out Gouzenko was in custody, and took over the security and oversaw the debriefing.

"Even so, some months later Mackenzie King stepped in during the ensuing investigation and ordered it halted. Why? who knows? . . . he said it had become a witch hunt for communists in the civil service. Personally, I think he didn't want a scandal to cloud his last years. And we know now that he had already gone bananas over the occult world. I guess he couldn't handle the existence of a real secret world. Anyway, he stopped the investigation cold. On the Prime Minister's orders, all the evidence from the Taschereau Hearings — held in camera — and the evidence collected by the Special Branch was sealed away in a vault for the next twenty years; until 1968 when the Security Service started up Operation Featherbed.

"The Taschereau Hearings? Operation Featherbed? You'll have to get that stuff from someone else. But those are the historical determinants that set the scene for S's arrival.

"So in 1952 he shows up, cloaked in the aura of MI6 experience, and he has all the jargon of the intelligence game: d.o.b.s, L.O.B.s, illegals, deceptions, all that kind of crap. And it sounded as professional as hell. It was a case, you know, of bullshit baffles brains. Well, maybe that is a bit simplistic. Because even then S was one of the most glib, plausible, and intelligent people you could hope to talk to. He seemed to have an encyclopedic knowledge of just about everything from the Boxer Revolution to the writings of Immanuel Kant. Which is no mean ability in Ottawa. I have always maintained this city is overrated. Because, despite the high concentration of intelligence, university graduates, and thinkers, all gathered here to service the federal government, they are for the most part simply a bunch of technicians. You know their kind of thinking: They'll readily make the bomb, but don't bother them with the moral problems of how it will be used. Really, I challenge you to go into any government department here and provoke a serious discussion on any of the more profound aspects of the problems they are dealing with, be it justice, energy, or foreign policy.

"The technicians make up at least half of the civil service. The other half are simply political flunkies, people who have won their jobs through the patronage system of the Liberal party. I often think this is what it must have been like under the Czar Nicholas — all those bungling middle-class people desperate to hold on to their jobs and their lifestyle, without any interest or even perception of the underlying problems of our time. They just don't have the equipment.

"In all my years in Security Services, working on the Soviet and other communist desks, I never once heard any of my superior officers, aside from S, have anything intelligent to say about the capitalist system, much less provide a clear analysis of Marxism. But that is what we were charged with: to block the pene-

tration of our institutions by agents of Marxist governments. Makes you think, doesn't it? I mean, in the
long run, how can they lose?

"This brings me to probably the most important
quality S had going for him. He definitely was not
welded into the RCMP officer establishment, which
projects the kind of attitude we describe as the cavalry
officer mentality. Sometimes it is known as the
Genghis Khan Horde Syndrome. The traditional
RCMP executive officer loves to see men in uniform,
the more uniforms the better. I know you are going to
find this difficult to believe, but it wasn't until about
1962 that intelligence officers were allowed to go to
work in civilian clothes. And for a while the cavalry
officers insisted we wear a 'civilian regulation dress'.
Can you imagine such bullshit? Blazer, flannels, and
hat. I remember one summer we were the only guys in
the city of Ottawa running around in straw hats, all of
the same distinctive 1920s design. I'm sure the KGB
has us all pegged. So you can see quite easily how such
attitudes would tend to set up barriers between the
headquarters executive and the operations staff.

"As a civilian member of the force, S didn't have to
put up with a lot of the crap. He had his own style: the
same tweed jacket year after year, grey baggy English
pants. He wore slippers in the office. But more important, in contrast to the cavalry officers, S was extremely affable. He had a good sense of humor, and was
generally pleasant to work with. We were thrown together socially many times and I can tell you he can be
a charming and entertaining companion.

"Did he protect his own men? That's a good question. Well, let's say he was an astute politician. If you

were a winner, you were protected. If you were in a bit of trouble, you know, slightly wounded, he tended to find his way out of his responsibility toward you by damning with faint praise. But he was not an outright assassin. Administratively, he achieved his ends by guile, rather than by bloodletting. And you see butchery wasn't really necessary, because very quickly he had established quite a following. He had become overnight, so to speak, *the resident authority on counter-intelligence.* In no time he went from assistant to the officer-in-charge of B Branch, counter-espionage; to the officer-in-charge of the Soviet desk; to the post that he really chiselled out for himself: director of counter-espionage — which carried the rank of superintendent. Not bad for a guy who had started cold as some kind of analyst in the research section, eh?

"Now to say something else about this man: He was an absolute sponge for work, and I've seen a lot of grinders in my time. I'm a bit of a work addict myself, but this guy left us all behind. Literally everything that came out of B Branch, from the most important correspondence on active case files, down to the most trivial Telex concerning travel information about some Soviet diplomat, passed through S's hands."

* * * * *

The Au. has been able to corroborate these facts from several other sources. Despite his affability, despite his humor, S had no colleagues — only underlings. Molonski: "I worked for him for fifteen years, but the only time S ever asked me for an opinion was if I thought it might rain that night." Even if you put aside the possibility that he was working for The Other Side, another Philby, any hard-eyed administrator would soon realize that such a man was not contributing to the development of intelligence officers or to the efficiency of an organization.

No letter or memo, no matter how inconsequential, left B Branch without S's scrutiny. And he would always, *always,* put his imprint on it. Even if it was only to make a minute change in grammar or composition. The fascinating irony was that his handwriting was illegible. (Molonski again: "It looked like something carved on the outside of an Egyptian tomb.") Let the psychiatrists make of that what they will. But DV claims the RCMP had to keep a young woman around B Branch, "some senior officer's idiot daughter" who in every other aspect was witless except in her ability to decipher S's handwriting.

Such a heavy bureaucratic hand, the insistence on seeing every piece of information, produced inevitable bottlenecks. Then, the enormous dependence he created in that role must surely have robbed anybody else of any initiative. How did he accomplish all this between eight and four-thirty? He didn't. S was in at seven every morning and never left before six-thirty, often later. And, as far as the Au. has been able to determine, never took a holiday all the time he was in the RCMP, certainly nothing more than a long weekend.

The other activity that kept S busy and in town was his Ottawa trapline. He didn't really travel the cocktail circuit too much. He worked at a lower key: a few quiet drinks in the evening, dinners with small groups. He certainly dined out a lot. Knew all the first-level apparatchniks. Certainly, he knew a lot of people in the federal government at all levels. It was, Molonski says, "the best trapline on the force." Because of who he was and because of the people he talked to, he had access to information that cut across all government departments. Deputy ministers, as such civil servants are wont to do, probably confided in him more than they would their own ministers, in keeping with the old public service adage: "Ministers come and go, but deputy ministers go on forever."

Would S begin investigations on the basis of information he picked up on his trapline? It is hard to determine. He could pass along information or he could start an investigation. He was in such a pivotal position it was impossible to know whether he had begun an investigation on his own initiative or was carrying out a verbal command from a superior officer. And that was something else about S. Behind the amiable facade, he was, by all accounts, an intellectual bully. He had the ability to intimidate people with the idea that he knew a great deal more than they did. DV: "He always made me feel that he had the secret info, the real inside dope. He was able to mystify the intelligence game without ever making it corny."

Again, it worked both ways — on his superior officers and for people who worked for him. For example, until Letourneau came on the scene, the directors of Security Services were out-and-out cavalry officers, career men bucking for Assistant Commissioner or Commissioner. They knew absolutely nothing about intelligence work. What's more, they didn't want to. This seems to be the consequence of having a police force organized along military structures of command. An officer would come in from running the maritime division of the RCMP, where the biggest problem had been the sale of cheap booze smuggled in from the French islands of St. Pierre and Miquelon in the Gulf of St. Lawrence. Then wham! He is our man against the KGB. (The Au. has evidence that it made for some interesting managerial crises.)

So the first objective of the security services directors would be to keep things as calm as possible — do their tour of the post without any embarrassments on the record. It was a disaster for the record book if you allowed the Prime Minister to be photographed shaking hands with the leader of a Soviet trade delegation, who could be later identified by the press as a KGB spy thrown out of Britain two years earlier.

There were a couple of cavalry officers who tried to milk the position for their own publicity. DV: "We all remember Assistant Commissioner Smellie. Hounded some wretched postal clerk to an early grave. The guy had been set up in a deception operation by the Soviets." But their publicity-seeking attempts for self-aggrandizement always backfired. And so it appears that it was usually fairly simple for S to handle them. By all reports, he did it well and smoothly with overviews and slick reports that didn't tell them anything more than they wanted to know. He apparently did it with more finesse than his colleagues in D Branch, counter-subversion, the officers charged with surveillance of Canada's own revolutionaries. Molonski: "I remember a briefing when the officer from D Branch presented the 'threat list', those people and organizations who had the supposed potential of overthrowing the government. The commanding officer of security services suggested, with a certain mild sarcasm, that perhaps it was about time D Branch dropped the survivors of the MacKenzie-Papineau Battalion from the list — you know, the Canadian contingent to the Spanish Civil War. Poor old buggers were even by that time in their seventies.''

That, it seems, was the extent of involvement for most of the "cavalry officers" in the real workings of intelligence; a mild remonstrance to show that they were not complete fools. The rest of the time they could then devote to mess dinners and being absolute martinets about dress and discipline. DV: "It was really an ideal situation for a mole. A mole? It's the term for an intelligence officer who starts out on one side, digs down, and burrows deep into the heart of the intelligence organization he was given the responsibility to penetrate.

"And you see, S could pull the same sort of smooth technique on his subordinates. For example, I would be sitting on a guy for six months. All kinds of manpower and equipment from the Watcher Service tied up, at great expense, to keep the suspect under surveillance; finally I would decide that this was just another deception case the KGB had pulled on us while they were doing their real work somewhere else. I remember one case very well. I received a message from MI6. A young Polish guy, supposed to be an agent in Polish Intelligence, which automatically means that he is fronting for the KGB, was on his way over here, a legal immigrant. How does he do that? Turns out that his father, now a chef at the Chateau Laurier, somehow got out of Poland twenty-six years ago, before his son was born. The chef and his wife had already agreed to split up. But he is a good sort. He sends money back home to help her out. She keeps up a once-a-year kind of correspondence.

"Suddenly, twenty-six years later, the son wants to come over to join the father he has never seen. The old man says, 'Well, okay, but I don't know that we are going to have that much to talk about. I've got my own family now. But what the hell, blood is thicker than water and if you want a start in this country I'll get you through the immigration hassle.' If you're an immigration officer and you look at that, it looks perfectly normal: Hard-working immigrant family trying to pull together. Victims of the Cold War. But I'm an intelligence officer, and I say that's a perfect setup, an absolutely ideal way to slip an agent into the country. The only way you can prove this young guy is not a blood relative is for him to take a blood test. And the minute you do that, you blow the fact that you already *know* who he is. And you don't want that. What you're after is his contacts, his target, and so on. And even if he is a blood relative, so what? He could still be a trained agent.

"I pick up this guy from the moment he enters the country. He spends a few days with his father, then sets up in a room. He gets a job as a medical lab technician. I stay with him all the way. I know who his girlfriends are, what they talk about. I know that a couple of times a month he makes it with the boys. The guy can't fart without me knowing it. But nothing, absolutely nothing. No contacts. No suspicious trips. For a guy who has just broken out from behind the Iron Curtain, he is living one of the dullest lives imaginable.

"So I suggest to S that we haul this guy in for interrogation, give it to him hard and heavy, bring the operation to a head one way or another. We've spent enough time and money. So what does he do? S leans back in his chair. Puffs thoughtfully on his cigarette for a couple of minutes. 'Do you recall the 1938 Hong Kong Telephone case?' he asks.

" 'Well, no,' I reply.

" 'Well, there you go,' he says, 'Damned fascinating.'

"And for the next forty-five minutes he gives me the history of the 1938 Hong Kong Telephone case in such convincing detail, and how it relates so concretely to the case I'm working on, that the only inescapable conclusion is to go back and keep the suspect under surveillance for another six months."

* * * * *

DV's stroll has brought us to Rideau and the canal. Across the street the Chateau Laurier, its Count Dracula architecture at once ridiculous and gloomy, veils its interior promise and tradition as a hotel of naughty nights for politicians in the federal capital. DV, one hand jingling some coins, saunters across the broad concrete pavestones to the steps that will take us down to the canal path. A panhandler, who seemingly came from nowhere, confronts DV. He is an Indian, friendly and smiling. He silently and adroitly reaches out and covers DV's coin-jingling hand with both his own. For a moment the two of them are locked like that — to an onlooker it would seem that neither man wanted to make the next move, but was curious as to what the other would do. The Indian is a husky man, almost as big as DV, and is dressed in jeans, bush shirt and a worn, brown leather jacket. With the easy grin of a natural con-man, he opens DV's hand and picks out a quarter. "See this?" he asks, in a soft lilting voice in which the consonants are clipped and rolled. And he holds up one face of the coin so it glints in the light of the street lamp. "Das a caribou. You kin feed one helluva lot of people wit one caribou. My people done dat for hunnerds of years. But see this?" He turns the quarter to display the Queen's head. "Only thing gonna happen to you there is you gonna get screwed." He chuckles with a deep gurgling sound, eyeing DV expectantly. But DV gives nothing. He is suddenly the impassive Southern Ontario farmer, tolerant, but refusing to enter the game. With a vague cool smile, he thanks the Indian for the story and drops the change into his palm. The Indian pockets the money and turns away in one gesture. But in the fraction of a second before he turned away, they looked into each other's eyes, and the look that passed between them left the strong impression with the Au. that both men really knew each other. And that the exchange was spontaneous theatre between two actors who knew their parts so well that they derived a deep sense of irony and satisfaction that went far beyond the immediate appreciation of the audience.

"Do you know that man?" asks the Au. as they descend the steps that lead to the canal tow-path. But DV has wrapped himself in silence, offering the impression that he is observing, rather than listening. They pass the boisterous noise and lights of the pub in the National Arts Centre, where people in brightly colored summer clothing sit at long wooden tables, drinking beer out of large plastic cups. Students are mixed with tourists. The lights and sounds cast reflections across the shimmering surface of the black canal water. The atmosphere is animated but without tension.

Early September in Ottawa makes the residents forgive and forget too easily the brain-numbing harshness of the winter months. September evenings are long and somnolent. The air moves softly, caresses the face and bared skin. For those who live downtown, the Rideau canal is the focal point of these evenings. The paths and parkland that stretch beside the canal become crowded with strollers taking the evening air. Families crowd the park benches until long after their children's bedtimes, finally surrendering the benches to couples who will linger until the early morning hours. Cyclists, singly or in groups, peddle lazily along the path. Here and there, runners, dressed in flimsy shorts and undershirts, lope silently through the knots and clusters of people.

If DV sees all this activity around him, he does not absorb it. His vision retreats with a seemingly constant energy into his obsession. To ask questions about S is simply to set in motion the conditioned reflexes; the channels of demand and response have become worn smooth in his mind. The examples, stories, and flotsam of circumstantial evidence are marshalled and moved to the front of his thoughts as efficiently as a computerized program.

The Au.can only wonder at what point all the factors had come together to trigger this preoccupation in DV. He makes a mental note to seek out DV's wife, to interview her and attempt to gauge the personality DV projected before he became seized by the career of S. He starts to drift off, envisaging what kind of woman she might be, the questions he would ask. With a start, the Au. realizes that he had for a moment tuned DV out. Is it a temporary state of saturation?

". . . The way the work is compartmentalized in Security Services, it is always difficult to get a feeling of what is going on with other cases. The very nature of the job rightly prevents other departments, other desks, from knowing in any detail cases that are being handled. This overview, of course, is the responsibility of the headquarters branch of the Security Services, which in this case was S. We were like puppets on a string, S the master puppeteer."

When things go wrong in an intelligence officer's work, it becomes very difficult, complicated. He has to talk to somebody, but is sworn to secrecy, so he can't go home and talk it over with his wife. He has to find someone else who is also sworn to secrecy. Inevitably, he has to talk to another intelligence officer. There's nobody else.

In the fall of 1969, DV was the assistant to the desk officer of the Soviet Desk, B Operations, A division, a man the Au. will refer to as Wilson. One warm evening DV offered Wilson a lift home, but discovered his superior wasn't immediately interested in reaching his destination. Wilson's wife and children were away for a few days on a family visit and he had the urge to break out of his daily pattern — at least for a few hours.

Intelligence officers don't like to be seen talking together in bars. Besides, DV needed more privacy than would ordinarily be found in such a public place. They bought a case of beer and drove out to Gatineau Park, where they found a secluded spot, broke open the beer, and started to talk. DV: "He was a good desk officer, actually ten years younger than me. One of the new young Turks. He had come up through the ranks and was sent to university by the Force. Instead of taking the usual law courses and accepting the blinkers that go with it, he was lucky enough to get into a political science and history course at the University of Toronto." From there, Wilson had apparently plunged into graduate work in modern political history. But more important, he had a curious mind, an awareness that allowed him to apply what he had learned outside the Force to his intelligence work.

It seems that Wilson was probably one of the first officers to start challenging S at an intellectual level. DV: "I used to love his memos. They would begin with phrases such as 'If history has taught us anything . . .' And he had enough gall to continually question orders. 'How does the fulfillment of this operation assist us in the realization of our political values?'

"Perhaps it doesn't sound like much, but then we have never been exposed to a steady diet of RCMP-report language in full flight." (Molonski: "It can reduce the Second Coming of Christ to a really boring affair.")

"So there we were in the Gatineau Park, drinking beer in the moonlight. What's going on? we're asking ourselves. We work our asses off but nothing is happening. In intelligence work you can be wrong a lot of the time, but not all the time. We go over all the operations that have gone belly up over the years; the double-agent cases that have gone wrong; surveillance operations that seemed so promising and then just petered out; contacts with Soviet Embassy types that hadn't gone anywhere. Be more explicit? Okay, the conventional wisdom in intelligence is that nobody 'serious' is run out of an embassy. A 'serious' is an illegal, someone with a phony nationality. Remember Lonsdale? Sets himself up in a legitimate business and pursues his spy career without ever going near the embassy of his real country.

"The practical contradiction is that world events move too fast to put all your intelligence work in to such long-term operations. An 'illegal' can take five to ten years to set himself up as a model pillar of the community, before he can start to be really useful. So in addition to illegals, intelligence organizations must use their embassies for faster results. The embassies provide access into the country, a secure base, and if the intelligence officer is an accredited diplomat, the worst that can happen is that he is declared *persona non grata,* and he catches the next plane home. So that's why so much time and energy is spent watching foreign embassies, identifying the intelligence officers working there, and keeping them under surveillance. That's what E Branch, 'technical and surveillance', and the Watcher Service, is for. These are mainly civilian employees of the RCMP, men and women, picked to look as unlike an RCMP officer as possible. No six-foot-two, cleancut farmboys from Saskatchewan. If they have you under surveillance you would never know it. They range in type and size from the four-foot-eight greaser who looks like he should be pumping gas to the demure-looking girl-next-door type.

"The members of the Watcher Service have the faces of most foreign diplomats memorized and carry photographs of the ones they don't. They're all excellent drivers, drive everything from laundry vans to taxicabs, with the most sophisticated radio equipment. You've seen those antennas on the Soviet Embassy? The KGB uses them to try and jam the communications between the vehicles of the Watcher Service. It's funny, eh? the KGB knows more about the Watcher Service than Canadians do.

"S was the man who created and developed the Watcher Service, it was always under his direct command. He always kept a very close check on its activities and personnel. At that time there were perhaps about a hundred of them. S knew them all. Every once in a while, all this surveillance would turn something up: Someone from the Soviet Embassy gives a Canadian citizen a large sum of money to buy real estate, or a business. Aha! we would say, a support system being prepared for an illegal. So you watch this Canadian like a hawk. Or say E Branch turns up the information that a Czech officer from STB, that's their outfit, has something going with a sweet young thing in Montreal. Well, you work on it. From behind the scenes you help develop the relationship. You unobtrusively feed perks into the situation, make sure the woman has legitimate access to money so that even she doesn't know where it is coming from. It just happened in this case that a recently deceased male relative was a former RCMP officer. It was easy to leave her some money from his 'will'.

"Pretty soon this Czech is deeply in love with this woman, life has never been so good. You work on it some more. If he likes her, he likes Canada even better. He starts to give out little signs, indications that he would like to stay in this land of milk and honey. But how can he do that? He is a Czech, an intelligence officer; heavy stuff, probably nobody would believe him, think he was a KGB plant. At that point the intelligence officer who has been developing the case moves in: 'Sure, we would like you to stay. Think you're a terrific guy. Leave it to us, we can fix it.' You build that for a while. Get him committed in his own mind that he is going to defect. Then you pull the switch. 'Listen, you don't get anything for nothing in this world, right? Everyone has to work for happiness. You want Canadian citizenship, a special pension? Right, well, this is what you have to do.' The object is to turn him around. Send him back to get high-grade intelligence.

"Okay, so all this stuff is going on. But nothing really develops. The guy who bought the real estate with Soviet money does nothing but develop a chain of dry-cleaning stores — works day and night at it. The STB officer is turned around. He starts working for us. He accepts a temporary reassignment to Prague, for microdot training, he tells us. There is no doubt in our minds he is genuine. We never see him again.

"Finally, at about two in the morning, after hours of going over case after case like that, all with similar results, Wilson says: 'Okay, here's what we're going to do. I'm going to assign you to an analysis of all these cases. Let's see if there is a common problem, something that will give us a clue to what is going wrong. But this is just between you and me. I'll cover for you. You know, of course, I have no authority to do this, so we'll say you're doing the research to prepare an update of the operations manual.'

"I spend the next four months in one of the reading rooms. Wilson keeps calling the files down for me. I concentrate on twenty-five cases and examine another hundred. I start to think I'm going to go out of my mind. I must have read about five million words. I guess you have never seen an intelligence report from the Watcher Service? 'Suspect hesitated before crossing Elgin Ave. at five thirty-two P.M. Took a white handkerchief from his right hip pocket, blew his nose. Returned same handkerchief to left jacket pocket. Checked his watch on left wrist. Crossed street. Scratched right earlobe with forefinger of right hand. Entered Elgin Ave. smoke shop at five thirty-three. Picked up *Maclean's* magazine with left hand, turned to page twenty-seven, began to read illustrated article on topless Manitoba dancers organizing union . . .' S had these guys so well trained they drowned us in a sea of trivia." DV falls silent again, and stays that way for a long time, or at least so it seems to the Au. who, aware that he is perhaps at the point of discovering an extremely important piece of evidence that is possibly fundamental to his investigation, is hard put to maintain his passive role.

Those one hundred and twenty-five reports did not tell DV and Wilson anything they did not already know: a) that each operation did not result in "effective intelligence advantages" — to use the jargon of the profession; and b) that S was the "puppeteer who pulled all the strings." In despair, DV called again for the twenty-five principal files. And then something quite remarkable happened, one of those strange turns of fate, accident, the kind of incident that surrealists describe as the *moment explosive,* the point in time when the searcher, quite by accident, is confronted with that which he seeks.

DV: "I'll never know how they turned up or how they got there, but when this stack of files was dumped on my desk, two very special files fell out. They were, in size, color, and design, only slightly different from our own, but noticeable all the same. I was on the point of calling back the constable who had brought them — they were obviously misfiled — when I idly opened them up. I was staggered. They were CIA files. Reports of two cases. I could only come to the conclusion that one of the CIA men had been over using our files — they have always had free access to our case histories — and had somehow left them behind and they were gathered up by the clerks."

Sounds incredible? Not really. The Au. knows an inspector who absent-mindedly put a top secret file on the roof of his car, then climbed inside and drove off, to leave all those secret documents blowing down Laurier Ave. For the next two weeks, people kept wandering into RCMP headquarters with pieces of paper marked "Top Secret, For Serpent Project Personnel Only", innocently asking, "Does this belong to you?" No, the really remarkable aspect was that both files were directly related to what DV and Wilson were looking for: The first was a report that two CIA officers had witnessed RCMP security services Sergeant David Blake, while supposedly shopping in an Ottawa supermarket, receive a package from an attaché of the Soviet Embassy: *RCMP Sgt. Blake pushed his cart alongside that of Military Attaché Bogakov. Without exchanging words or signs of recognition, Bogakov casually placed two large-size boxes of breakfast ce-*

real in Blake's cart. Blake, in turn, slipped a packaged
toothpaste in Bogakov's shopping cart . . . .

The two CIA men evidently followed Blake to his car in the parking lot, and at gunpoint relieved him of the cornflakes boxes. Inside they counted fifty thousand dollars in used Canadian bills in various large denominations. The money was returned to Sgt. Blake with the information that his transaction would not be revealed to any authority in the RCMP or Canadian government. He was also advised to resign immediately from the RCMP Security Services. In return for this advice, Sgt. Blake was happy to inform his two CIA counsellors that *the toothpaste tube he had deposited in Military Attaché Bogakov's shopping cart had the name of a STB officer written inside the package.* (It was of course the name of the Czech officer, whose love affair DV had "tended like a rose garden.")

The second file was more enigmatic. It was a report on the curious death of the CIA station chief, Mark Henderson, who two years earlier had been found dead, seated in a chair in front of his television set. The set was still on and a half-finished meal sat on a tray on the table in front of him. The autopsy showed that he had choked on a piece of steak gristle. His body was discovered shortly before midnight by S who, on his way home, had happened to see the lights on, and stopped by. The two men were apparently more than professional acquaintances. DV: "They played poker together once in a while. S had been over there for the odd evening drink. It would not be unusual for him to drop by like that."

The night has suddenly turned darker. And, at least to the Au., it seems the previously warm air has taken on a late-night chill. The dark green-black water of the canal itself seems to offer some unknown and brooding menace. DV's "stroll" has brought them as far as the Bronson Bridge. There is very little park beside this stretch of the canal, and the tow-path is temporarily deserted. DV turns away to lean against the metal pipe railing and contemplate the murky waters of the canal. It is into this scene that a slim woman of perhaps twenty-eight appears. She is dressed in a loose white cotton dress that flutters around her ankles. She is walking, pushing along a red and green woman's bicycle by its handlebars. Even under the dim light from the street lamps, it is immediately obvious that this is an extraordinarily beautiful woman. A long Arab face, olive skin, and black hair that falls in thick curls to her shoulders. The woman greets DV with a smile. In a few minutes the Au. is introduced. With a pleasurable shock of surprise, he realizes that this is Krista Gollner. A few more words are exchanged and then she mounts her bicycle and rides away.

* * * * *

As a footnote to this long ambulatory conversation with DV, and his revelations of Wilson's display of initiative in this first "unofficial" investigation of S, it should be pointed out that DV was "eternally grateful" to Wilson for hauling him off the RCMP's Great Homosexual Search, about three years earlier. DV: "You've never heard about that, eh? It is one of the truly grimy chapters in Security Services history. I was attached to that investigation, I think, as a disciplinary measure. It was a fall-out from an incident a couple of years earlier in Moscow. Apparently our ambassador there was gay, and he had worked it out that several of his boyfriends in External Affairs were posted to Moscow with him. Well, there they were, having — not to put too fine a pun on it — a gay time, when the roof fell in on them. Various KGB types started to corner them in bars, show them pictures of themselves in bed with Russian homosexuals, and demand certain non-sexual favors in return. It was the typical blackmail setup. The ambassador tried to hush it up, but the CIA tipped us off to what was happening, and the boys were brought home. That would normally have been the end of it. But the cavalry officers in the force went into this incredible and vicious over-reaction: 'All homosexuals have to be weeded out from positions of trust in the public service.' I think it was probably one of the most personally destructive operations carried out by Security Services.

"Personnel officers, who are really for the most part informers, fingered guys in their departments who they thought were supposed to be 'a little, you know' as they would say. These poor guys would be confronted by a couple of RCMP officers, and here is where it was so stupid. The honest guys who said, 'Sure, I'm gay, so what?' lost. Their department heads immediately demanded their resignations; they had 'confessed', you see. The ones who denied the accusation, knowing the investigators would have a hard time proving anything, were allowed to stay on, although I'm sure many were shunted into dead-end jobs.

"My God, what a witch hunt! They even commissioned some mad psychiatrist — a guy who wouldn't recognize a homosexual if he woke up with one — at

Carleton University to build what was quickly labelled the 'fruit machine'. It was a sort of lie detector machine, and there were all these questions, if you gave the wrong answer it triggered a current, lights and signs started to flash. What? Okay, well, maybe there weren't lights, but you get the idea. And you can understand how thankful I was when after about two months of this kind of work this guy Wilson from the Soviet desk managed to pull me off that investigation. I have always thought that S had something to do with the Great Homosexual Hunt. It had his trademark. Probably put a flea in some cavalry officer's ear. From S's point of view, it was simply another great way to tie up a few more intelligence officers and Security Services resources.''

SECTION III

The Au. feels that he should pause here and answer the question that has possibly by now arisen in the reader's mind. How does a writer become involved with an investigation of intelligence organizations without being in some way part of one himself?

It is a suspicion that no longer surprises the Au., because in the course of his long investigations he has been alternatively suspected as a CIA agent by members of the paranoid and extreme left, or as an RCMP intelligence officer (by the ex-CIA employees he has interviewed). Neither is true. And although the Au. is aware that by simply stating "that is not true," no matter how often and emphatically, does not necessarily, make it so. Intelligence information, except in wartime, seldom has much to do with hard facts. Mostly because the information is rarely put to the test of combat realities. Therefore it is inevitable that a vast amount of intelligence information is based on that which would *appear* to be the most plausible, the most convincing, within the given context of the intelligence-gathering activity. With the intention of "convincing" the reader with the "most plausible" information, it is necessary to go back to:

November 19, 1973, Santiago, Chile, The Blue Danube Restaurant on the Calle Monjitas (where the Au. has been sent by a magazine to write about conditions in the aftermath of the coup d'état that overthrew the government of Salvador Allende). The interior of the restaurant — the ubiquitious German wine cellar with rough wooden tables and chairs, wide-planked floors and heavy-beamed ceilings — reverberates with the sound of some twenty male voices singing, no, bellowing, Fascist victory songs, sometimes in Spanish, more often in German; for these young men are members of the *Patria y Libertad,* the Fascist party, which has flourished in various guises, first within the German-Chilean community, and then, as it was nurtured under the care and attention of the CIA, recruiting its members from the upper class — the landowners of the south, and residents of Santiago's *Barrio Alto.* The *Patria y Libertad* became the instrument through which the CIA performed the "dirty tricks" — assassinations, bombings, kidnappings — to reach its objective of "destabilization of the Chilean society."

The bellowing young men now begin to sing the opening lines of the Fascist hymn — "Cara el sol, con la camisa abierta." The Au. sits on the other side of the wine cellar with two young men and a woman. It is a testament to the courage and coolness of the Au.'s companions that they can sit and regard the fascists with such benign smiles and pretend now and then to mouth words to the songs, but in truth the young woman is softly singing their own song: "Companeros . . . toward sunlight, toward freedom . . . See the procession of millions . . . Surge forth without end from the night . . . till your demands and your longings flood the whole sky out of sight. Shatter the yoke of the tyrants that cruelly torture the world . . . Over the mass of the workers let our blood-red banner be unfurled . . ." for my companions are *Miristas*, members of the *Movimiento de Izquierda Revolucionaria.* "It is MIR that has been the vanguard of revolutionary activity in Chile for the past five years," says the young woman. "Allende has had his opportunity with his experiment in social democracy, now it is our turn."

Brave words. Chile lies torn open. Four weeks after the CIA-manipulated *golpe,* President Salvador Allende, the first legally elected Marxist president in the western hemisphere is dead; the presidential palace is gutted, the walls pockmarked with rocket and fifty-calibre machine-gun fire. In the centre of the city, eight thousand leftists have been imprisoned in the National Stadium. The corridors in the complex below the grandstand of the smaller Hippodrome Chile on Avenida Indepencia run with the blood of victims. The change rooms have become the temporary torture cells for those men from the police and armed forces who will later form the dreaded DINA under General Augusto Pinochet.

Santiago is a city that lies in the grip of a sickening fear. The *toque de queda,* the daily curfew, begins at seven in the evening. Sometimes it is, without warning, brought forward to five. The buses stop even earlier. Without transport, the workers rush to get home — any way they can.

It is in the evening that Latin American cities come alive. The citizens circulate through the cafés and restaurants, visit families, to exchange the news of the day. But now because of the curfew they are isolated, locked up in their homes, fearful. And because the military junta controls the media, there is no explanation on the television or radio for the machine-gunfire in the night; nor for the presence of the bodies dressed in overalls, executed in the National Stadium, and dumped at the bus stops to terrorize the workers coming out of their homes in the morning. There is no report on the union leaders who disappear. There is only the mute evidence of corpses thrown — hands tied behind the back, a bullet hole in the back of the head — into the Rio Mopocho. The corpses float, drifting with the current, until they wash up on the banks of the poblaciones — the slum districts of the workers.

Now, even the middle-class who clamored for this coup so that they could be given the right to govern with the privilege of their class are terrified. Because the military, its snout covered with blood, has proclaimed that "democracy is no longer necessary. The military will rule for the next hundred years."

"Will you kill everyone, the forty-three percent of the population who voted for Allende?" asked General Alberto Bachelet who, loyal to the constitution, refused to join the junta in their *golpe* and is under house arrest. "No," replied Pinochet. "It will only be necessary to kill a hundred thousand of them."

General Bachelet, interviewed by the Au. the same day he was brought by the Miristas to the Blue Danube: "The military junta know what they are doing. It will be more than fifty years before socialism regains its strength in Chile."

"That's him. The one who looks ill from too much drink. He sits with his hand against his head while the

69

others sing,'' says the Mirista to the right of the Au. ''He is the CIA agent who controls the files and is visited every day at the American Embassy by the RCMP officer.'' Mirista to the left of the Au: ''In the first six months of Allende's government, two of the *compañeros* infiltrated *Investigacciones,* so that on the day of the *golpe* they were able to inform us that police detectives loyal to Allende had destroyed the police files on political activists. The military have some. But the best political files are now held by the CIA in the American Embassy on Calle Augustinos. The woman: ''Now we have to go. The *toque de queda* begins in forty minutes and we have work to do tonight.''

(Au: Within a year all three Miristas were dead. General Bachelet, half-starved and sick after long months of torture, died in February 1976 in a Santiago military prison cell.)

What to conclude from these grim reports and blurred images of violence and death in Santiago de Chile? . . . that the RCMP daily gave the CIA the names of those men and women desperate to escape Chile through the neutrality of the Canadian Embassy? Is such collaboration ''small beer'', to be shrugged aside, as it is by an editor at the Toronto *Globe and Mail?* But then the tall, slim RCMP officer who drank late into the night with the Au. in his room at the Hotel Crillon on Ahumada did not think so. He saw himself as in a Kafkaesque nightmare, standing on a shore, ''daily washing my hands in the river of blood that sweeps past.''

At four in the morning, hopelessly drunk, the RCMP officer, who met every day with the CIA agent who controlled the political files in the American Embassy, stood at the hotel room window. He listened to the heavy *dum dum dum* cadence of a fifty-calibre machine gun in the distance, then suddenly shouted: "This is history. The moral descent of Chile, of all Latin America into the Middle Ages, on a slide built by American foreign policy and the CIA. You can't write about this. You can only write news stories. Leave this to the historians." And then more quietly: "If you want a story, go home and write about the KGB penetration of the RCMP. That's only a story." Then he staggers to the bathroom, to vomit into the toilet.

* * * * *

For the Au. the road from that Santiago hotel room to the role of unofficial and unauthorized witness to what appears to be the final downfall of Superintendent S, has been long and complex. There have been many side excursions into explorations of the structure of the Security Services, and attempts to analyze the role it plays in our society. A great amount of time and much effort was put into making contact with those journalists and civil servants whose responsibility it is to do business with Security Services officers.

The Au. would have liked to report that it was some sudden dramatic encounter that led him to S. What really happened was that he had developed a friendship with an older and established journalist, a man who, in his own words, was "learning how to die." Cancer had begun to devour his body, telescoping his perspective and collapsing his future into a matter of months. One afternoon when the pain seemed to have temporarily subsided the Au. joined the veteran journalist in his garden. It was one of those sunny spring afternoons, the weather, and the explosive flowering growth of the garden all in ironic counterpoint to the journalist's own existential plight. But the sun warmed his already frail body, and the Au. was deeply moved by the realization that the journalist chose to savor the moment rather than to mourn its implications for himself.

They had a long wandering conversation about women, children, and learning how to write. The journalist already knew about the Au.'s growing fascination for the Security Services, and perhaps because he sensed his own time had run out he began to talk animatedly, and in detail, about his long experiences with the SS. At one point the phone rang inside the house and the journalist went to answer it. When he came out several minutes later, he held a photograph in one hand. It was one of those group portraits of a dozen men taken after a special Security Services training class. Without explaining how he had obtained the photograph, the journalist pointed to a man in a tweed jacket: "Let me introduce Superintendent S, now retired. I interviewed him nine months ago in England. The RCMP believe he is, or was, a double agent —for the KGB — but nobody, it seems, has been able to prove it. A problem of mainly circumstantial evidence, I understand."

Three months later the veteran journalist was dead. But before he died he had introduced the Au. to DV. And that is when the pursuit of S began in earnest — for the Au. that is.

When his wife once asked him why he wanted to spend all his time in this manner, the Au. would only say, "Because it's a good story." But secretly he hoped that he would be able to discover within his project a meaning — an encounter with an experience that would perhaps, at very least, clarify those truths he had already learned about men and women.

* * * * *

The Executive Assistant: ''What more can I tell you about this man that you don't already know from reading the quotes that he offers to newspaper reporters for all those banal interviews? You know, the ones that use the weary analogies to professional sport: 'The Prime Minister is the captain of the team, and we're trying to win the Stanley Cup', or 'You can't stop skating in the third period . . .' I can give you the ones that don't make the press, the *macho* clichés he uses to exhort his staff to more efficient organization: 'Lay your plans and plan your lays,' or to greater effort: 'Even in a gang bang the best sperm lays the egg.' He is a hollow man, I tell you. He is the original one-dimensional hollow, hollow man.

''Why do I hang in there? Because the cabinet is still the cockpit. It is the closest a 28-year-old guy like me, an EA, can get to whatever power there is in this country. Because, you see, in Canada there isn't enough power to go around. Historically that sort of analysis wasn't officially accepted around here until guys like the sociologist John Porter put the academic seal of approval on it. But really any Ottawa cab driver could give you the same analysis on a six-dollar ride from the airport. In our country there are no opposing or balancing institutions. It is more like a pyramid with finance, business, the judiciary, and the civil service, all folded into the base of the Liberal Party. Socialism for the elite, we call it.''

For the past half-hour, the Au. has been watching the executive assistant to the Solicitor General toy with a glass of beer without ever raising it to his lips. ''Yes,'' the EA admits, ''I'm not a juicer. In fact I never touch the stuff, just go through the motions. Surprised, eh? Yeah, I know, boozing is supposed to be a parallel activity to my job. But I'll tell you something that might sound even stranger. I quit drinking when I started this job two years ago. I remember that I kept looking around me in amazement. I saw all these experienced men drink under pressure. It reduced them to something pathetic. They're supposed to be the most powerful honchos in the land. Instead they get into the sauce about four or five, sometimes it's lunchtime. By six-thirty it's like your average annual office party, only worse, all these middle-aged guys — when you mainline on booze and power, it does weird things to the head — acting like randy Calgary bulls, wrestling the help down into the nearest leather couch.

''At first, I kept asking myself, is this my future? Well, if it was, I didn't want to know about it. To paraphrase Chairman Mao's slogan, it was sort of like looking down the wrong end of a double-barrelled shotgun; the corruption of power and booze. So, I thought if I cut out the booze it would somehow take away one barrel, and I could concentrate on the barrel· with the power. Yeah, of course it fascinates me. Power fascinates everybody. But for me, the hook is the political philosophy of power. However, there is one thing you learn up here very fast, and that is whereas collectively these guys are fairly awesome,

74

especially when they can concentrate and get it together long enough to get the machinery of the state cranked up to move on a specific objective — remember Sartre's *Question de méthod?* I keep trying to find ways to bang dialectics into the SG's head; to tell him that 'dialectical refers both to the connection between objective events and to the method of knowing and fixing those events.' But a person would make better progress with that beer waiter over there.

"And that's what I'm getting to: taken individually, these so-called powerful men are intellectually at ground zero. Have absolutely no comprehension at all of political philosophy or the psychological presence they should inhabit within the consciousness of the people. Except for a few individuals, it is unexplored territory. These guys have replaced political principle with the image; the shoddy, real or imagined, media image. That's why the PM finds them so easy to handle: a little Burke stirred in with a pinch of Machiavelli, a paraphrase of Sartre, and they fall in behind him like a herd of stunned buffalo. Ever see a buffalo staring at the cover of J. K. Galbraith's *The New Industrial State?* Well, there you have it. Can you imagine in our day and age that Galbraith is required economics reading for the cabinet? My God, I mean it's hardly enough to keep the mind alive! I don't agree with very much of what goes on over in Treasury, but they're right on when they describe the PM as an economics illiterate."

Overwhelmed by his feelings of cynicism and disgust, the EA lapses into a tight fidgety silence, snapping and unsnapping his metal watch bracelet and constantly pushing a lock of hair out of his eyes. The Au.

75

has to spend the next few minutes gently nudging the EA away from his black vision of the nation's political leadership to the objective of this interview: the internal problems of the Solicitor General's department.

The EA: "Yeah, I know about the Superintendent S business. Weird stuff, *heavy* as the children say. The minister has had me try to find out the score, but it's a bit like going fishing for lake trout in July, you have to get your hook deep, really deep. On the surface it has all the markings of being nothing more than an internal bureaucratic struggle. Get below that and it has all the potential of having the kind of dynamite that can blow a government out of the water. What do I think personally? Well, from my point of view I think that S is one of the bad guys, that after he retired from the Force, he intended to just drop out of sight, disappear. And then one fine day his memoirs would emerge from somewhere like Prague, published courtesy of the KGB presses. But hell, I can't give you any proof of that. It's just my reading of the situation; or, more correctly, of what the RCMP chooses to tell us.

"I can really only tell you what I know, what I witnessed down there in Washington with the minister. We were having some preliminary talks to do with exchanging US and Canadian criminals so that they could serve time in their own countries. The Americans weren't particularly interested, the imbalance — we have a lot of American criminals up here — was in their favor. So instead of coming home, the minister wants to live it up a little. Against his better judgement the RCMP guy down there — he serves as the liaison with the CIA — takes the minister and myself to a bash for a group of intelligence officers. Have you ever noticed how high intelligence officers like to live? They always know the best restaurants and whorehouses. As a group they can outdo politicians at the trough, and that's saying something. I was along as the babysitter to the SG.

"I never did figure out what the celebration was all about, but it was being held in a suite of four or five rooms at the Watergate, no less. Very spiffy. Enough booze to fill a swimming pool. Lots of expensive food being trundled around on glass and silver wagons. Must have been about a dozen tall, slinky, absolutely gorgeous ladies, obviously hired for the evening, drifting around over the pile carpet; definitely a class bash. I got the impression that some grateful arms dealer had organized the party. Because there were an awful lot of strange types around who described themselves as being "in armaments procurement," the kind that seem to operate at the outer edges of the diplomatic circuit. I bumped into a couple of guys I had met before as they passed through the US Embassy up here. Chaps who had been vaguely introduced to me as Internal Revenue Service types, but who spoke too many languages and were too up on politics to be anything other than CIA — I mean they drift through Ottawa all the time and you get so that you can spot them in their pyjamas, they all have that pinched Jesuit look in their eyes from too many years at Notre Dame University.

"At first these guys seemed a little taken aback at seeing me there with the SG. But they seemed to be quite happy to sit around and chat and laugh at the minister's jokes. I guess if they had any idea of what was going to happen they would have got us out of there right away. What did happen? Well, we had been there about an hour and the minister had lined up on one of the slinky ladies, disappeared down the hallway with her for an hour and returned with that smug well-screwed look I have got to know fairly well. Immensely satisfied, he got another drink and seated himself in a comfortable chair with the apparent intention of joining what seemed to be a drunken and intense argument. However, the minute the SG sat down, most of the others sized him up balefully and drifted away. There is no doubt that we were being made to feel very definitely unwanted and the RCMP guy who brought us there was making all kinds of obvious noises implying that we should leave. He even came over and growled in my ear: 'Listen, I've wined, fed, and had the sonuvabitch laid, now get him the hell out of here.' But I'd recognized from the experience of previous performances that it wasn't going to be that easy. I whispered in the minister's ear that we had to prepare for the next day's cabinet meeting in Ottawa. But he waved me away. When the SG wants to party he becomes fairly insensitive to the affairs of state, let alone other people's needs. So I convinced the RCMP guy to stick around and wait for the right moment.

"We sat down on either side of the minister, facing the only two guys who hadn't walked away from him. One of them was really drunk; had to sort of prop himself up in the corner of the sofa — he was a strange skinny guy, looked more like a scientist. The second guy was just mean drunk. Our Mountie had earlier identified him as a CIA colonel who used to be the station chief in Bogota or some godforsaken place like that, and was now director of the Latin American section in Washington.

"The SG thinking, I suppose, in his own dumb way, that he could establish some common ground with these two weird birds, started to talk about the Bardesio affair. But he did it all wrong, sounded as pompous as hell, and the cop from Bogota began to bait him. It got worse. The RCMP guy and myself were aghast, tried to shut the minister up; but the SG's pride was touched, he was going to show these goddamn gumshoes that it's the politicians who run the show. He ended up by warning the CIA colonel that he, the Solicitor General, was on top of the situation, and the CIA had better not try to ice any more Latin American agents in Canada, because 'the Canadians aren't going to put up with this shit any more, so the CIA had better stop trying to treat us like some half-assed banana republic like Ecuador, or by God . . .' At this point the skinny scientist type, who had been owlishly silent all this time, leaned out of the corner of the sofa and in a thick German accent blurted out: 'You moron, you think you're in charge, but you don't even realize your director of counter-espionage was a double agent all this time. Why do you think he was interrogated by . . .' He never got to finish because the colonel, with a move that came out of nowhere, cold-cocked him. I thought we were the only ones in the room, but I turned around to find my two 'Internal Revenue' friends coldly regarding the whole scene with a very fishy eye. The SG himself was, to put it mildly, shaken — something had obviously gone very wrong — and even angrier. 'Ce n'est pas terminé,' he muttered and stormed out of there.

"The next day he was still furious, but full of energy. I think he realized that possibly for the first time

SECTION IV

What of S? DV maintains that he hasn't seen S since their return journey to Ottawa. The Director General of Intelligence, himself a former military man, met them at the airport. "The plane parked away from the terminal. The DGI was there, no one from the force, just a couple of thugs from military intelligence. I recognized one of them, a chap who had been over to Northern Ireland for 'interrogation training.' We know what that means. They took S away in a limousine with Canadian Armed Forces plates. I haven't seen him since. Bastards never even offered to give me a ride downtown. I had to find my own cab.

"When I got to my place, I downed two stiff belts, and then collapsed on the bed. When I woke up twenty-four hours later, I still had all my clothes on." DV also claims not to know where S is being held. And despite the most intensive efforts, the Au. cannot locate S or determine the exact conditions under which he is being held, detained, kept incommunicado; nor can he accurately choose which, if any, of these terms are applicable.

By now the reader must be aware that the Au. has come to share, at least in part, DV's fixation for S.

This fascination provokes the question: is it possible that the Au.'s obsession fits within the same perspective held by DV? The Au. has spent a great deal of time thinking about this. He cannot yet make up his mind, but is almost convinced that for DV, S exists as a symbol of "reflective consciousness," — S, in the role of double agent, represents an anarchic freedom that DV can neither share nor experience. And, although DV most certainly *respects* S, his conscious perspective of S cannot seem to move beyond the narrow moral framework of "deception and betrayal."

Is it precisely S's alleged ability to play the game on both sides without being trapped that makes his role, his whole persona, even more *seductive* — if that is the right word — to a plodder like DV?

Where does the Au.'s obsession fit in? It is, possibly, no more than a sophisticated projection of DV's. Only the Au. would like to think that his interest is not so much with what the man has done, but has moved deeper — to an examination of this supposed "freedom", and what motivated S to act. How real was S's "liberty?" It is a question the Au. has pondered for some time. But how to penetrate S's interior life? how discover if he ever looked back at certain stages to ponder the ambiguities of his existence? The Au. wonders if S ever tried to define those courses of action that might have offered him a greater realization of individual liberty. Has he been able to say to himself: "It was a mistake, or even, "I had no choice?" Or did he so consciously alienate his "self", so lock himself completely into a role, a formula, that reduced the interior energies of his life to a series of subformula and subroles to the extent that his existence became totally predictable? If so, should not S then be treated sympathetically, as a victim? It is possible that we must view S as a man who began as an idealistic revolutionary, an infiltrator of police systems that oppressed the masses, but who was then caught up by the waves of history and left beached, isolated, with no resources but to go on playing the only game he knew. To this DV has a practical reply: "Nonsense. He was and still is an intellectually arrogant man. He may have started to act from a sense of revolutionary idealism, but he figured he was going to outwit us all at playing the game."

Does DV mean *all* in the universal sense? Perhaps the game of intelligence becomes so spacious in the psychological views that it embraces, that it permits the participants — once they have forgotten or become disillusioned about the causes that were the rationalization for entering the game — to abandon the role of *Soldier Under Orders* and take on the persona of a lone guerilla, an anarchist of the intelligence world. It is one of those ideas that has roots in historical precedent: The Ievno Azeff Affair. From 1901 to 1909, Azeff — a brilliant and remarkable young Russian from an impoverished Jewish family — was a leader of the "Battle Organization," an anarchist-terrorist wing of the splinter Social Revolutionary Party. At the same time he was plotting and carrying out the assassination of the Czar's chief ministers, he was a highly paid *agent-provocateur* of the Ochrana — the Czar's secret police. Azeff carried out the assassinations as efficiently and as energetically as he betrayed his comrades. But so well did he manipulate both sides that even an official investigation by the Bolsheviks in 1917 could only conclude: "It is impossible to say which side he served

83

best." Azeff died a year later at the age of 49, diseased and in poverty, after spending the years of the First World War imprisoned by the Germans as "a dangerous radical."

DV is wary of this historical comparison. He refuses to elaborate and will only say that for another dimension of S, the Au. should speak to Hazelton, or better still, Hazelton's wife.

* * * * *

Hazelton is a well-known journalist. He is the editor-in-chief of a rabidly right-wing Toronto tabloid, the heir of all those tabloids that emerged after the Second World War and thrived in the atmosphere of witch hunts and cold war tension. Claiming to represent the working people's interests, Hazelton and his staff reduce the most complex political issues to the narrowest and most simplistic interpretations. Using the "tits and crime" formula as bait, these stories are sandwiched between exploitative photographs of women and bizarre reports of crime and passion. The result, although journalistically regressive, is commercially rewarding.

In person Hazelton conveys the impression of a man with a cool and austere mind working efficiently from deep within a bloated body. He is too intelligent a man to try to hide behind the same trite arguments offered by the publisher: "We are successful because we give the people what they want." For Hazelton, son of a famous American political family, with an education and experience of life that is unemployed in the meaness of his present occupation, the rationalization is political. "It is the vehicle with which to combat socialism and support free enterprise.'' And wisely, he will not be drawn into discussion of the more grubby and corrupt activities of the property developers who form the board of directors of his tabloid. (The Au. does not want to suggest that the owners of other metropolitan newspapers have a more profound moral grasp of their function. For perhaps in the end the difference is only one of style, a surface observation of the more conventional restraints, while more subtly but steadily reinforcing the vested interests of class, sex and money.)

Also a journalist in television, but less well known, is Hazelton's wife or, to be more precise, his separated wife. ''We just don't seem to have got around to the finalities of a divorce, although it must be ten years since I left him.'' She is a warm and instantly likeable woman — the kind of person one meets and feels at ease with, simply because she is able to invoke an immediate dispensation of the customary artificial barriers between strangers. ''What do I think of his newspaper . . .? Oh, let me see . . . the best way I can sum it up is to tell you this story I heard the other day: People who read the *Globe and Mail* think that they run the country. The readers of the *Star* believe they *could* run the country. The people who read his tabloid don't give a damn who runs the country as long a they have big boobs . . . No, I don't think it's a vehicle for fighting creeping communism. That's a pretentious joke. As a vehicle it is there only to serve as a voice for the property developers who don't like legislation that will control their speculative profits — it's as simple as that. All the red-baiting and conspiracy hunts just sell newspapers.

''No, he wasn't always that way, at least not that I

could perceive, but then I was very young and naive. He is fourteen years older than me, you know. When we first met we were working in the same Ottawa newsroom. Certainly a more classy milieu than those dummies on that tabloid. It was my first job after university. He swept me off my feet, literally. By the time I came down to earth, there we were in Russia. He, as the newspaper's correspondent, me as a freelancer, wondering what on earth I was doing there, and why I was pregnant. Life was not turning out as I had planned. It was the kind of predicament that really only another woman could possibly understand and sympathize with. Not that I had much time to sort it all out. Being in Moscow was of course fascinating. Life was a blur of activity — Russian language classes, the diplomatic cocktail circuit, the Bolshoi, interviews with all kinds of amazing people, especially educators; it was my specialty. Even then I was fascinated by the Soviet's education system. I remember that I wrote articles predicting that very soon every third scientist in the world would be Russian. But editors laughed at me, thought that I had gone soft on communism. Well now it has all happened and I don't think anybody remembers those articles. It may sound wistful, but it's true, you know, journalism is written to be forgotten.

"Ah yes . . . and then there was Natasha. I was wondering when you would get around to asking about her. I was so dumb, never suspected anything. Frankly, I liked her. I would probably have liked her even more if she didn't have the ability to make me feel like such a klutz. Although I'm sure it wasn't intentional on her part. It was just that she was so cultured, so poised, *so* gracious. She was also ten years older than me. I was definitely outclassed, a bubbly twenty-four-year-old, struggling to hide her own lack of confidence, trying to keep up with a brainy, handsome, — yes, he was even slim then — older husband. My God, I still groan inwardly when I think of how gauche I was.

"Natasha was our guide-cum-interpreter. But she quickly became more than that — and I don't mean just in the way that makes you smile. You have no idea how dependent you can become on someone like that, especially in a place like Moscow. She could cut through all the language problems, the bureaucratic red tape, and she was always able to get tickets to the Bolshoi or anything else that you wanted to see. Yes, no doubt about it, she was very impressive. Of course, at that time, I had no idea of the resources she had to call upon.

"As I say, I never realized anything was going on between them. And even when he sent me the cable from Beirut — I had come home to Toronto for the Christmas holidays — I was so dumbfounded that it took me quite some time before I could take it seriously: 'Do not return to Moscow, have eloped with Natasha.' Only *he* could use the word 'eloped'. To cut a long story short, Natasha apparently had all these forged passes and documents that got them out of Moscow to a port on the Black Sea. It was all kind of a James Bond adventure. Somehow Natasha got them onto a cargo boat to Beirut where they took refuge in the French Embassy. From there they made their way to Paris. That's when he phoned me and asked me to get in touch with S. They apparently had some prearranged method of communication. Because I only had to tell S to expect a phone call. Yes, they had known each other in Ottawa. Hazelton explained to me that he couldn't leave Natasha because he thought the KGB would probably try to kidnap her, but that when he got home he would explain everything.

"Well, he had more people to explain to than just me. His publisher was furious; he knew that he would probably never get another correspondent into Moscow. External Affairs was a bit put out. They viewed the whole adventure as well, vulgar, a bit unsavory. However, in the face of all this S got Natasha a minister's entry visa, and they flew to Toronto together. For my part, I was, to put it mildly, more than ready to drop out of his life and start determining my own future.

"Somehow — he can be very charming — he managed to placate everybody and left for the USA to take up his next post as the Washington correspondent for the paper. The idea was that Natasha would join him there as soon as she got a US visa. But it never happened. The US immigration authorities kept putting them off. Hazelton apparently had S behind him all the way, but it wasn't enough. So he began to make a nuisance of himself with various Washington officials. Finally the publisher called him back to Toronto for a special session, a 'man-to-man talk'. He later told me that when he walked into the publisher's office, he was astonished to find S there, the Ottawa CIA station chief, and the FBI liaison officer.

"They had, they told him, bad news. They thought that he should give up his attempts to get Natasha to Washington, as she was never going to get across the border. Because, you see, they had this conclusive information that Natasha had a husband — we had always understood she was single — who was a famous KGB colonel, in intelligence circles, that is; and it was he who had signed the passes that got them from Moscow to the Black Sea. Also, the whole 'secret voyage' to Beirut had been carefully prearranged.

"Well, of course, he was quite shaken. He immediately broke with Natasha, and I don't think he has ever been the same man since. I am convinced that the whole incident marked him with his hideous paranoia that seems to have become the driving force in his life and is responsible for his involvement with Toronto's right-wing extremist thugs. Not only does he see a red under every bed, but also *in* every bed. Natasha? . . . Oh, she stayed around for a while. Took some courses at the University of Toronto. An RCMP car followed her back and forth for a couple of years. I don't know exactly where you could find her now."

Hazelton refused to meet with the Au. Evidence of paranoia? But in the course of a telephone conversation he agreed to read the Au.'s notes from the interview with Hazelton's wife. A week later the Au. received in the mail a plain brown envelope that contained two pieces of yellow copy paper, double-spaced: "You might think these nitpicking points, but I have always appreciated your reputation for accuracy.

1. It must be evident from the circumstances that my wife did not leave me, but that I left her.
2. I never used the word "elope" in the cable to my wife.
3. The passes that got us to the Black Sea port of

89

Odessa were not signed by Natasha's husband 'the KGB colonel', but forged by Natasha in my presence.

4. S's role is not as clear as my wife implies. My impression is that S, a long-standing friend consistently acted out of human consideration rather than professional objectives. It seems to me that she is suggesting that S obtained a minister's entry permit for Natasha in the pursuit of some undefined intelligence objective.

5. I suppose that it is possible that Natasha had been "trained and waiting" for this alleged espionage role. However my conclusion is that her training — which she had openly confessed and described to me before we planned our escape — had fitted her for the low-level interpreter/informer role commonly assigned to those who work with foreigners in the Soviet Union. Her duties were to keep the KGB informed of my movements in Moscow, my contacts with Soviet citizens, and any vulnerable personal habits the KGB could exploit to their own advantage. None of which would groom her for the high-level role of information-gathering one would expect of an agent intending to penetrate Washington circles.

6. I have had a great deal of time to ponder her motivation, and I concede that there might have been a degree of opportunism on her part — but I am convinced that it was the direct result of wanting to escape the dreadfully oppressive and deadening existence led by the majority of those under communist dic-

tatorships. Finally, there is the personal question — not to be lightly dismissed — for after all, it was the basis of our personal relationship. I have never doubted that Natasha had genuinely fallen in love with me. And although it might seem rather lame to say it now, I had never committed myself to a long-standing relationship with her. In any examination of our feelings it was always evident that it was more important to her than me. To be honest, for me the whole event was undertaken in the spirit of adventure — the objective of which was to extricate a charming and cultured woman, who desperately wanted to escape, from the oppression of a communist society.''

So much for the extra dimension to S; or had the Au., intent on exploring the interior life of S, misunderstood DV? Possibly DV had meant that the Hazelton affair was simply a deeper dimension of S's alleged betrayal. And that S, in his role as double agent had been attempting to ease Natasha into Washington, and could do so on the pretext of his longstanding friendship with Hazelton.

* * * * *

''Listen, they tell me you're on to something very interesting. Perhaps I can help.'' S held somewhere in secret custody, the Au.'s enquiries, the SG's indiscreet activities in pursuit of an explanation for S's early retirement, have all begun to generate tiny tremors of energy through the Security Services. Journalists like Atkinson, who work closely but unofficially with the police, are extremely sensitive to such minor shock waves, and their reactions are often complex. The initial response to "there's something going on" is, as Atkinson freely admits, to determine, "How can I use the story — assuming I can get it — without burning myself first, or the contacts I have with the force." Stories for journalists like Atkinson are seen basically as springboards, and in the past he has used them well. They have brought him from the small western newspapers, to the eastern metropolitan dailies, then into national televison. It is a recognized and accepted route, along which the pitfalls are many. Few have survived the marks of passage as well as Atkinson. "A great deal depends on judging who you can afford to burn. I have always found the best question to ask is: "Will this take me to a position of greater strength — if it won't, then forget the story, let someone else do it." But overriding these primary considerations is the problem and promise of "the big story." The one that will vault the reporter into the star role that can be parlayed into a fat contract, or even sometimes into a well-paid sinecure in the upper levels of government bureaucracy. As long as the anxiety that he may be missing "a big one" persists, Atkinson must check out the possibility, and that is why he is on the phone now, alternately exploiting a youthful association with the Au. and then implying the "motherlode of information" Atkinson has gathered from his weekly luncheons with "my inspector from O Division" (Toronto division of the RCMP) will be available to the Au.

Through DV the Au. has some idea of how that

"motherlode" is obtained. At those weekly luncheons Atkinson informs on his fellow journalists, not really so much on *them* (although he often fills in information to complete the dossiers RCMP Security Services keep on all journalists) as on their contacts within government bureaucracies. Journalists are pathologically unable to keep themselves from bragging about their sources — it is the cachet that gives them status among their colleagues. Atkinson's currency consists of turning over to "his" inspector in O Division the names of the bureaucrats who become the confidantes of the press, the frustrated deputy assistants, and the disgruntled and passed-over department heads who can no longer forbear the stupidities of their ministers.

In time, thanks to Atkinson, the talkative bureaucrats find themselves shunted off into dead-end jobs, where the only alternative is to resign or use up energy trying to expand nonsensical work to fill the hours, relieved only by long liquid lunches commiserating with fellow dead-enders. In return, Atkinson gets bits and pieces of security gossip about politicians, or the opportunity to obtain "off-the-record corroboration" of alleged investigation into government corruption — his motherlode.

"Marvellous," says Atkinson, "my place at eight, Thursday evening."

* * * * *

Krista Gollner: "Physically, there was nothing unusual about S. Quite frankly, it was his mind that turned me on. He was always sensitive. But never in that brooding way. He had a wit that was whimsical, very charming. No, he certainly was not what I usually look for in a man in physical terms. And yet . . . there were some truly remarkable moments. Sensual moments I suppose you would call them. He would take my hair in careful handfuls, then gently rub them across my breasts.'' The Au. was quite undone by Krista's dreamy expression and the langorous way in which she absentmindedly caught her long black hair in one hand and gestured across the front of her blouse, a colorful garment that looked as though it might be from Guatemala.

The Au. has just come from his first interview with Krista and the above statement is not, of course, the first information volunteered about herself and S. Rather, it came after more than two hours of listening. And the Au. has to admit to a struggle here. He has already found Krista Gollner fascinating. More, he is strongly attracted to her. The problem in this report is not to present her so that her sensuality makes her the victim of a certain sophisticated voyeurism. No, she must be presented for what she is. And if Krista has entered into the fantasy life of the Au., then he must work through this to perceive a clearer image of S. Because for the first time the Au. feels that he is getting closer to S, that he is no longer just a figure in a landscape. Perhaps it is only the insights of a lover that can give flesh to the fleeting images we see as people. Their revealed sexuality suddenly makes them vulnerable; reduces them to an important banality: the flesh, still mysterious but no longer fantasy, expresses a certain commonality. Moreover, to see those around us as naked is often a relief.

Before going to meet Ms. Gollner the Au. put down

everything he knew about her. That is, all the information he had collected and his own observations from the single brief meeting with her in the presence of DV on the Rideau Canal bank. Age, a surprising thirty-five, but a woman who could easily pass as at least ten years younger. Tall, about five-foot-nine. Slim, perhaps one hundred and twenty-five pounds at most. Her skin, a pale olive, and the already mentioned black hair that fell to her shoulders in coarse heavy curls. (How to explain the Arab face?)

The Au. has learned that Krista earns her living as an interpreter, English/German/Spanish/French, on contract to the federal government. It is a job that pays her about twenty-five thousand dollars and seems to include a great deal of overtime. Her language speciality is Spanish and so naturally her work is most often with the Cuban delegation. From time to time she has work with the occasional group of West German businessmen, but they usually speak English so well there is little real need for her services.

DV says he checked Krista out with A Operations — security clearance — and discovered that although she has a Canadian father she has interesting "ties" with East Germany. "Her father is an old Canadian lefty, but her mother was German and had some ties with the German communist party." After the war, the mother took Krista and disappeared into East Germany. Much later Krista reappeared as a student at the Sorbonne and then at the University of Madrid.

For a while Krista had a job at the United Nations in New York, then spent two years in Washington working for the US government; because of this DV is convinced that Krista is CIA. "Nobody with a background like hers, that had those East German connections, could ever get a job in Washington. It all fits too well. Because then she turns up in Ottawa, and almost immediately has worked her way into the sensitive post in which she can keep a close eye on who is who in the Cuban Embassy and which of the Cubans have contacts with the Canadian government. You have to admit that it is an excellent position to know exactly what the Cubans and the Canadians are talking about.''

But then DV admits that he has nothing more than that to go on. And besides, the RCMP has never been interested in attempting to track CIA activities in Canada. There isn't even a CIA desk in Security Services. DV: ''Most of the officers seem to feel that the RCMP is a country cousin of the CIA and FBI, and are quite happy to keep the relationship that way.''

Krista Gollner did attract some Security Services attention when she developed a friendship (no one knows if it was any more than that) with Karl Kling, an international arms dealer who had fallen on difficult times and sought temporary refuge in Montreal.

DV: ''Kling was one of your tall handsome European playboys. He held an Austrian passport that showed his age as thirty-four. Young, but already a millionaire, he made it as an arms dealer in the Middle East and North Africa. His problems began in 1970 when he became the payoff man — some kind of CIA middleman — for the multinational oil companies who were paying ransom to keep the Palestine Liberation Organization from blowing up oil pipelines. The Israeli intelligence organization, the Mossad, became aware of Kling's activities and put a great deal of pressure on the Italian government — Kling at that time had made his headquarters in Milan — to force Kling out of Italy. The Mossad could have easily killed Kling, but they didn't want to antagonize the CIA unnecessarily.

"The Italian government's opportunity came on May 17, 1972, when Luigi Calabresi, chief of the political investigations section of Milan's police force, was shot to death by an unidentified assassin who escaped. Calabresi had been accused by a bunch of Italian anarchists of the death of a fellow anarchist. It was the same old crap, you know . . . This anarchist was supposed to have fallen or jumped from the window of Calabresi's office during interrogation. Three days later, the Milan political police search Karl Kling's apartment while Kling is at his office. The officer in charge of the search phones Kling to tell him that the gun that killed Calabresi has been discovered in Kling's apartment and that they are on their way over to question him. Kling, grateful for the sophistication shown by the officer and aware that he could spend up to two years in an Italian jail before charges are even laid, thanked the officer for his information and caught the next plane out of Milan. It happened to bring him to Montreal. He set himself up in a suite of rooms in the downtown Senesta Hotel. About eighteen months later, Kling suddenly dies."

Au: Kling's death certificate, available on request for a charge of $3.50 at the Registry of Births and Deaths reads only "natural causes" in explanation of Kling's sudden passing. Nor would the doctor reveal to the press the results of the autopsy. "We must respect professional secrecy." The Au. has been unable to find anyone who saw the body before it was cremated. An elderly couple, reported to be Kling's parents from Europe, were the only ones to attend the private funeral service. The day after the cremation, Kling's hotel suite was redecorated and the two stunningly beautiful women who lived with him had disappeared.

DV: "Who knows what happened? Maybe it was a heart attack. It could have been that the Mossad caught up with him, or even the PLO; there was some talk that he had double-crossed the Palestinians." But what was Krista Gollner's connection with Kling? DV: "Could never figure it out. She spent a lot of time with Kling six months before he died. Trips to New York, nights out on the town in Montreal. And Kling was a big spender, a class spender, always the most elegant restaurants. Then some newspapermen 'discovered' Kling's presence in Montreal, and wrote background stories about how the Italian police wanted him, but really didn't want him, in connection with the slaying of this guy Calabresi. When that happened, she slipped out of the picture. I think it would have looked bad for her job to have been publicly linked to such a notorious character. He used to carry all these business cards identifying him as a sales representative for several arms manufacturers. He once showed me a letter of introduction signed by a US Army general in the Pentagon. There was no doubt that he was heavily involved with the CIA and the US military. Perhaps she had an assignment to get close to him to find out what he wanted. Whatever happened, the Americans burned him off. They asked us to tip off the press that he was here in Montreal. Then, on one of his trips to New

York, he was turned back at the border. Finally they cancelled his US entry visa. That was about two months before he died."

It is easy then to understand the Au.'s fascination, for, by way of a short summary: here is a beautiful young woman, with an unconventional family background, an excellent international education, the acknowledged lover of the RCMP's director of counter-espionage, a suspected CIA agent, and at the same time, a woman able to enjoy the friendship of as bizarre a character as Karl Kling. So it was with no small sense of anticipation that the Au. approached the house on Fourth Avenue to keep his three o'clock appointment with Krista Gollner.

The huge maples and elms that line the streets of the Glebe were in their splendid fall colors. Blazes of red and orange filled the afternoon light. The imposing three-storey houses created a reassuring sense of quiet and permanence. Krista's house was set back in a large walled garden that would have been spacious but for the tangled and unkempt growth of plants and trees. The Au. followed directions. "Come around to the back," she had said on the telephone, in a light voice that carried no trace of her polyglot skills, but sounded instead as Canadian as the Prime Minister's wife, "and up what used to be the servant's staircase. You'll find me on the third floor."

She met the Au. at the door, smiling, dressed in a blue, heavily-embroidered loose Latin-American shirt over white cotton slacks. "I was just about to run to the corner store. Please come in and make yourself comfortable. I'll be back in five minutes." And then, with another reassuring smile and a wave over her shoulder, she was gone down the stairs, leaving behind a delightful sense of warmth and color that was enhanced by the sound of soft Brazilian music coming from a tape recorder.

The Au. could not, of course, sit down. His professional deformities and natural curiosity took possession and he wandered around the apartment, delighted at this opportunity to absorb the evidence the apartment had to offer. The living room was surprisingly large and sunny with windows all along the southern wall. The immediate visual impression was so rich it was a little overwhelming. The walls were covered with framed paintings, photographs, and wall hangings from Peru and Guatemala. There was a comfortable leather couch and two deep chairs, and behind them, an organized clutter of books and magazines crowded into shelves, which at closer examination revealed a system of groupings by subject: politics and economics; novels, mostly in French and German; several books on yoga. And then two or three shelves of books that could only be loosely categorized as "intelligence and revolution," several books on General Reinhard Gehlen, former chief of Hitler's military intelligence on the eastern front, later for the West German Republic; Philip Agee's book, *CIA Diary;* several assorted works on the British spies Philby, Burgess, and Maclean; and then two or three shelves of books on Latin American revolutionary organizations; among them Righard Gott's *Guerilla Movements in Latin America*. The Au.'s attention was distracted at that moment by the music on the tape recorder automatically clicking to a stop.

He wandered through the apartment: a short hallway

opened onto a small but obviously well-organized kitchen that had a dining nook built into a window. There were hanging plants everywhere. Just outside the kitchen door in the hallway, there was a bulletin board, one of those cork panel structures single women always seem to have in their apartments and to which they attach their memorabilia. On this one there was the usual assortment of snapshots, trinkets, several postcards in Spanish; one from Mexico showing a violent detail of an Orozco mural: peasants with guns, their shoulders draped in bandoleers, being urged on to fight by a bare-breasted strangely whorish-looking woman. Then the Au.'s eye was caught by an old sepia-toned photograph, more of a snapshot, really, of a dark semitic young woman posing rather self-consciously in what looked like an inner courtyard in which there were decorative Arab motifs on the stonework. The woman's loose gown could not hide her voluptuous figure. But what made the photograph so intriguing was the expression of animosity in the way the woman held herself. The Au. had the impression that, against her will — perhaps with promises of money — she had been talked into coming out of a dark, cool interior to squint against the sun into what must have been an early box camera. The Au. unpinned the photograph; written on the back, in soft, barely legible pencil, was the one word: Aleayh. He replaced the photograph and turned to a half-open door on his left. From where he stood, he could see the end of a bed and beyond that a window which opened onto a view of a smaller canal that fed into the Rideau.

The Au. was just about to enter the room when he realized with a start that a man lay asleep in the bed, half-covered by a blue and white striped sheet. He was a big man with pale fleshy shoulders. His face, partly turned toward the window, was handsome in a heavy, blond Germanic way. The Au. (who has to admit that he was seized by an unreasonable surge of jealousy and envy) returned to the sun-filled living room where, on hearing light footsteps on the staircase, he sat down on a leather sofa to flick through the latest copy of *Le Nouvel Observateur,* which lay on the table beside the morning's edition of the Toronto *Globe and Mail* and a German edition of Heinrich Boll's *Group Portrait With Lady.*

It was not Krista who came through the open door but, after a perfunctory light tap-tap, a frail white-haired man of about seventy who, if he was startled to find the Au. there, was much more able to contain his surprise than the Au. After an exchange of introductions, it turned out that the old man was Krista's father, "the old Canadian lefty." The Au. was interested and at the same time alarmed that this parental visit would intrude on the interview. But the old man had simply stopped by to drop off a letter for his daughter.

"Just tell her I left it here," he said, with just a slight trace of a soft Irish accent, and dropped the letter on the glass-topped coffee table; then he was gone down the stairs. Midway he must have met his daughter, and for a minute or two the sounds and words of a pleasant casual conversation drifted up the staircase. Just before their good-byes, the Au. caught the words, "your mother wants to know . . ." and his gaze drifted down to the airmail envelope. Torn open at one end, it carried the postage stamps of the Democratic German Republic. At that moment, Krista returned to the room. "So you met my father. He is a really wonderful old man. I must tell you about him when we have time. Do you know just a few years ago at the age of sixty-eight, he was spending three months in China and got caught up in the cultural revolution? Yes, he actually joined with a group of workers in a sit-down demonstration that took over the party bureaucracy headquarters in Shanghai. Isn't that amazing?" But without waiting for an answer, she asked: "Will you have some tea with lemon? Good. I'll bring out some snacks." The Au. heard the latch of the bedroom door being gently closed, and then the sounds of Krista busying herself in the kitchen.

It was not until they had chatted for some ten minutes about life in Ottawa — in which Krista confessed she no longer felt comfortable cycling along the canal towpath in the evening because of "The Stabber", an unknown psychopath thought to be responsible for several murders over the last few months — that the Au. started to push the conversation in the ultimate direction of S. "Do I have much contact with the RCMP in the course of my work? Well, I suppose the correct answer would be that we interpreters could have as much as we wanted. I mean there is always a certain pressure there. The Security Services officers on the Cuban and Latin American desks are continually asking us about which Cuban diplomat knows who, what sort of contacts they have with Canadians outside government departments. Some of the interpreters, especially those working with the federal government and Soviet bloc countries, are outright snoops — and don't make any bones about it.

"A couple of women have got themselves into vulnerable positions. One of them — she does a lot of work with me — began sleeping with a couple of the Cubans and of course the SS guys found out about it; it seems they even have videotapes, and so she is under a lot of pressure to produce information and party with them. She's a nervous wreck over it all, but she's caught and doesn't see any way out. She's divorced and has a couple of kids and needs the job. But for the rest of us, I would say that we play a fairly careful game. For example, when an SS officer from the Cuban desk wants to debrief me, as they say, I just tell them what happened during the course of my work. If they want anything more, I just don't know how to help them, and that's the truth.

"A couple of times I have been asked by SS officers to do favors; pass an envelope to a member of the Cuban legation, and another time I was asked to leave a cigarette lighter in a certain location — I suppose it had some sort of microphone in it — at a reception at the Cuban Embassy. My reply was that I would have to speak to my director about it and obtain his consent in writing. That made them back off. I must say they are persistent in asking me why I don't socialize. They seem to have this crude idea that if I jump into bed with one of the undersecretaries, who is really here for the Cuban intelligence service, that the guy is going to immediately tell me all he knows about the KGB presence in Canada. They've never been able to explain to me why the second should be a natural consequence of the first. It *is* really very strange, isn't it? A bit like witchdoctors attempting to divine the mysteries of the universe by watching the fumbling copulation of insects. I once asked an SS officer, the one who was the most persistent in his suggestions of what I should do to ingratiate myself with the Cubans, if I laid him would he, in reflex response, tell me what his job was all about, and reveal to me the internal mysteries of the Security Services? 'No, of course not,' he said. He was really quite shocked. The irony was that he couldn't even see the humour in the question.''

This very matter-of-fact conversation sailed on with many smiles, shrugs and animated gestures on the part of Krista, who did not seem at all ill at ease discussing the clumsier attempts of her former lover's underlings to entrap her in a Mata Hari role. While she spoke, the Au. suddenly had an insight into the lot of the footsoldiers of the intelligence services; and was left to wonder at the strange blundering lives they were reduced to lead by following policies that emanated from God knows what kind of fuzzy bureaucratic minds. Or in this case, was it really that fuzzy? Was this in fact the successful end product of S's alleged ability to maintain the RCMP counter-espionage services at an advanced state of stupidity? Intrigued, the Au. hesitantly asked if Krista had been under the same pressure during her relationship with S. ''Oh, yes, our 'relationship', as you so quaintly put it, didn't seem to have any effect on that sort of thing. I suppose there were actually very few people who knew that we saw each other, let alone that we lived together for six months. When I did complain to S about the Security Services tactics, he would just shrug and laugh it off, saying, 'Good God, when will those guys ever learn?'

''Why did so few people know about us? I don't know, really. It seemed to me that although he had a wide circle of acquaintances, I can't really say that he had any group of friends that he would seek out to spend time with. If he did, I didn't know about them. I had the impression that his real friends were women. And that there were four or five of us with whom he maintained a very close connection. He was by nature very secretive. And it was only after I had lived with him for four months that I actually found out about the existence of the others. I was deeply wounded, and quite obviously I couldn't handle it, because after a while I moved out. No, it was not because I demand a monogamous relationship. I don't expect it of myself. And S knew that I saw other men. I never hid it from him. Yes, he knew about Kling.'' (The Au. wanted to slip in the question to establish a pretext for coming back to Kling.) ''How to explain this to you? . . . S had a very intense sensual way of dealing with you, or shall we say, women? He is one of those middle-aged men who really hypnotize a woman with the kind of attention they bestow. And he *was* hypnotic: his stories were always fascinating and he had a way of regarding the world that was quite profound but never professorially earnest. I can say that he had the ability to bring out the very best in me — something I have never encountered in another man. For me the experience was so intense, so vital, that I just wasn't prepared to share it with anyone else, another woman, that is. A strange contradiction? Yes, You're right and even when I hear myself describing this to you, it makes my logical position even more tenuous. But then, it's the emotional contradictions that make us human, isn't it? All I can say is that being with him and having the knowledge of his other women left me feeling . . . manipulated. And that's not really the word

I'm reaching for, but I can't think of a more accurate one, so it will have to do.

"What were the other women like? I can't really tell you; I never met them. A couple of them would phone his house and leave messages, or ask for him, and were not at all perturbed that I answered the phone. One of them was evidently Quebeçoise, and we once had a long interesting conversation about Francophones in the federal civil service. I never asked about her work but it sounded as if she did something over at Treasury. We were supposed to have lunch together, but it was just one of those things that never happened."

The Au. was quite dazzled by the total picture presented by Krista. She sat, alternately curled or stretched out in the long, black, deep leather couch — the perfect frame for her Latin-American blouse and thin white cotton slacks, which could do little to hide a figure which was nothing less than perfect. Throughout the next hour of conversation, she talked openly and without hesitation, except when pausing to find the right word to describe a nuance of feeling and emotion. She talked for a long time about the many conversations with S — apparently these were the best times for her — when they sat and talked late into the night, articulating thoughts and ideas, exchanging experiences in their lives.

It is obvious that the affair was much more important to Krista than to S. The Au. can only come to that conclusion because he could not see how S could have otherwise let Krista leave without demonstrating some willingness to make her the central person in his life. Perhaps he did in fact realize how important she was becoming to him. Was it a lifelong bachelorhood that made him wary of such emotional contracts, or a discipline and a purpose that ruled out the importance of a personal life?

"Yes, I know that S is back — DV told me. Something about an internal investigation. It doesn't really surprise me. I mean he is such a complex man, it would fit into the kind of picture I have of him. I'm sure that if you put together one of those psychological profiles of S it would become readily apparent from the demands he made upon himself and the world around him that he would have to be the hunted as well as the hunter. But I'm also sure that the RCMP aren't going to be able to get anything on S. It seems to me that they've never established an ability to deal with the complexities of the intelligence game. Why do I say that? . . . Oh, I suppose I get it from various stories S told me."

At this point in the conversation, the Au. detected a slight tension in Krista, nothing more than a sigh, or a reflective pause as she gazed out of the window at the vista of maple branches festooned with autumn leaves that, here and there, let go of the twigs that held them and drifted past the window in a last blaze of red and yellow. It was truly a golden afternoon, a moment in time that demanded introspection and confession.

"What a wonderful afternoon, it has such a sad sweetness about it. It's the kind of day on which you end a love affair." And then she unexpectedly laughed and cocked an eyebrow at the Au., "or begin a new one." In the laughter that followed, it seemed to the Au. that there was both recognition of his interest and flirtation from Krista. And despite his middle age and the awareness of the man asleep in Krista's bed, the

Au. felt himself slipping. In a bid for firmer ground, he turned the conversation to Karl Kling. But after several gambits — in which the Au. revealed more knowledge of Kling than he really cared to — it became evident that Krista did not want to talk about Kling, and if she knew of his contacts with the RCMP Security Services, she was not about to disclose any information that she might have. But then, just as the Au. was ready to give up with a trite observation about "secrets carried to the grave," he was shocked by Krista: "Kling is not dead." And then after several moments of flat silence in which the Au. decided it was best to remain silent, she added: "If you like I can arrange a meeting, and you can talk to him yourself."

Why would Kling want to do that — to shed such a carefully contrived cover and reveal himself? The Au. can only surmise that Krista Gollner understands Kling as a man flawed by the kind of vanity that afflicts the most audacious criminals: what is the point in being able to commit the perfect crime and let it remain a secret? The same imaginative energy that creates the crime seeks its satisfaction from recognition.

SECTION V

The EA: "Let's paraphrase Machiavelli — one of the PM's favorites, if not his favorite political writer: The primary object of every elite, or ruling class, is to maintain the power or privilege; and the rule of the elite is based upon force and fraud. And let's acknowledge that the fraud does not always have to be an upfront conscious policy."

The Au. finds himself seated once again watching the fidgety energy of the brash young executive assistant to the Solicitor General. And although he finds the EA's know-it-all attitude and use of bureaucratic jargon somewhat tedious — principally because it is an uncomfortable reminder of the Au.'s style in his own immature years — he cannot help but admire the EA's courage in his willingness to talk and his absolute refusal to be intimidated by the political power and position of his superiors. More important, and it would be hypocritical to suggest otherwise, the Au. senses that cultivation of the EA and the implicit flattery in this attention will bring its own reward in the Au.'s search for amplification and verification of S's role.

"Okay . . . let's examine the policies of the government toward these objectives. In the last few years we have seen excellent examples of both force and fraud. The brandishing of force was the War Measures Act in 1970. The police force threw four hundred people in the slammer, when all they really wanted was fewer than a dozen terrorists. The fraud was the plethora of funding programs for youth, the unemployed, and the poor, to give them the illusion they were participating in the democratic process. What! . . . you can't really believe that the PM has or originally had a sincere social conscience? I mean you actually believe that he was affected by all that hippy-dippy crap about an alternative society — 'the influence of his young wife.' That's all media bullshit. In the first place, his wife is nothing more than a gorgeous young woman from a moneyed family, whose understanding of an alternative society never went deeper than experimentation with an alternative *lifestyle* — there's a great deal of difference there. Besides, it's obvious in the way things have turned out. She is really just another jet-setter in search of the golden life and she'll undoubtedly find her feet on the deck of some oilman's yacht. Why did he marry her? I guess it just proves he's human. Listen, why do writers marry so often and unwisely?

"Secondly, to answer the point about the PM's supposed social conscience, this guy is probably the toughest, wiliest, most elitist politician we've ever had, and that *is* saying something. Because contrary to conventional thinking, we've had quite a few *pistoleros* running this country at various stages in our history. And like all of them, he has been consistent with the historical pattern: 'Be harder on your own people than in dealings with other countries.' Okay, so why

111

all those fraudulent programs? Consciously or unconsciously, he realized that when he went into his first campaign as Prime Minister, he didn't have a real base.

"As far as the voting public was concerned, he was nothing more than a media darling — which can often be the kiss of death, given how fickle those bastards are about political issues. So he had to build himself a base in the hearts and minds of the people. How did he do it? He did it in classic liberal-democratic form, by going out there and promising all those suckers — remember the PM's Just Society slogan — that they were going to have participation in the political democratic process. All the time knowing goddamn well how *he* was going to run the country which, as we have seen, has little to do with participation. But anyway, the whole country geared up, remember? The flower children wanted government-funded back-to-the-soil communes, and at the same time free access to the most medically advanced abortion clinics. Even those technically alive cadavers in the Senate were revved up. You had senate commissions investigating the media, sciences, poverty. And there were other royal commissions, investigating the arts, foreign investment, the status of women, and so on.

"The effect of all this, then, for your average elitist ruler, was quite marvellous. First of all, it siphoned off the energy of discontent that is always building up in an elitist society — with all those energetic brainy young people running around, interviewing, writing reports, and presenting recommendations. Second, it corrupted them. *They got used to the money!* One could almost make that Cabinet Directive No. 1: *Get them used to the money!* I don't know of any one of the under-thirty group who gave up the $20,000-a-year jobs when they saw the fresh new policies they had supposedly been hired to administer begin to wither on the vine.

"At an organizational level, all of those radical groups collapsed when the government funding programs ran dry. Because after a couple of years, once the PM realized he had established his political bridgehead within the population, it was time to cool out the level of expectations. Besides some people were going a little too far. They started to understand the process of what was really happening, of how they were being co-opted. In other words, they became politicized, started this really dangerous stuff: demanding community control, workers' control, redistribution of income, the sharing of wealth and resources, all the rest of that 'commie-pinko' stuff which is an anathema to a liberal-democratic society and extremely threatening to the elites that run it.

"And that's where the RCMP comes in — it is an essential element of the state apparatus that controls the population. Keep in mind that the PM has always been chairman of the Cabinet Committee on Intelligence and Security. That's also one of the reasons the RCMP brass hate him so much. He is always giving them a bad time about their obvious incompetence. At the same time, he recognizes that they are an organization that must be brought to heel — not so much for the good of the state, but rather for his own political purposes. Also, theoretically speaking, the RCMP is in the best position of any organization in this country to pull off the classic *coup d'état*. It is a heavily central-

113

ized para-military structure that controls policing in all but two provinces. And even there it has jurisdiction over a whole range of federal responsibilities. As well, the force enjoys a certain popular myth of competence, fairness and discipline. So you see, and I repeat, *in theory* it is in the optimum position to take over the country, given the right political circumstances.

"But *in practice,* the Security Services function as an apparatus for controlling dissent. In the late sixties they did what all secret intelligence organizations do when their purpose is to protect the elite — which of course controls the large non-political centre: the SS infiltrated the extremist right, not to destroy but to turn it against the left. So that's why in the early seventies, you had all these fascist thugs running amok, attacking Jews, blacks, Pakistanis, and any other racial minority. They had been led to believe they had police immunity. How do you do that? You let them break in and steal files from student activist groups, or groups trying to organize the poor. You get them to turn the files over to right-wing news editors — like that guy Hazelton in Toronto — who in turn will give them back to the SS. That sort of manouevre gives our little Nazi groups the idea that they are part of the police process and consequently immune to prosecution. Why else would the SS use those amateurs to do break-ins? I mean, they've got a whole branch of specialists in that kind of activity. Guys who could come into my apartment while I was away for the weekend, take apart the ceiling, install a few bugs, and then put it all back together without my knowing any difference.

"The second strategy against dissent is the informant system. This is a very strange country, you know. On the surface you would think that we were a people who, because of our history, our participation in a war against fascism, and our internationally known position against 'totalitarian police states', would despise squealers. But the SS couldn't operate without its system of informers. And a lot of it is not even on a direct contact level. Do you know, for example, that the Immigration Department in Toronto receives about two hundred letters — mostly anonymous — every week, denouncing or betraying illegal immigrants?

"The SS informers are everywhere. Their prime targets are the unions and university campuses, institutions that have historically created and cultivated dissent as a function of their social responsibility. In the seventies the union leadership of the Quebec Federation of Labor couldn't go out for coffee without the SS knowing about it — one of the confidential secretaries in the union head office was an RCMP informer. And of course all union information is turned around and selectively fed back into the corporations through what is known as the 'Ottawa Information Switch.'

"What would S have known about all this? Everything. His baby was B Operations, counter-espionage, and all this other stuff we have been talking about comes under D Operations, countersubversion. But S would be at meetings all the time at the headquarters committee levels with the Director General of Intelligence and the Assistant Commissioners of the Force. So, yes, he would quite simply be a party to all the information, and policies of 'destabilization' and control of dissent. Also, don't forget he was the guy who over the years created E Branch, the technical assistance

115

and surveillance specialists, so sure he would know about all the illegal break-ins and buggings. He dealt with those guys every day.

"Would the DGI and the Assistant Commissioners know about them? My reading of the situation is that the Assistant Commissioners would pretend that it didn't happen, and if a job were bungled and was blown, they would be mad as hell and want to fire everyone connected with it. Where the DGI instead, especially in the case of Letourneau, would endorse it as a necessary policy of his secret police. And if the job was blown, became public, he would try and cover for the guys involved. It's my suspicion that that's the difference that led to Letourneau's resigning from the force.

"Would his leaving have anything to do with the interrogations of S? That, in the words I wish my minister would use more frequently, is something about which I do not yet have enough information to comment. But I *can* tell you this. The Solicitor General and the PM have started into a dangerous game of poker with the RCMP Security Services. They are both convinced that they have been lied to about S. And so they have instituted a secret three-man Royal Commission of Inquiry, with an MP from the Liberals, the Tories, and the NDP. Everything in camera, of course. It's to try and smoke out what the hell is going on in that labyrinth of intrigue and incompetence that is the ambience of the Security Services. I'll tell you something else, too. They've allowed S, because he is no longer a member of the Force, to hire a lawyer — one of your smart, heads-up young Toronto radicals. A today kind of person. It's the best card the PM has played so far.

116

The SG's idea? . . . You have to be kidding! He couldn't dig himself out of a snowbank, even if you gave him two shovels and a kick in the ass to start him breathing."

* * * * *

The Au. can now introduce an informant who cannot be identified by his initials or by physical description. He must remain like those non-persons who are used on "investigative television programs," in which the character being interviewed remains only a silhouette, the face shadowed, the voice range and accent altered by the electronic process.

Unable even to reveal the circumstances that led him to this invaluable source, for to do so would instantly betray a sworn promise and perhaps inadvertently lead to possible identification of the informant, the Au. will refer to him simply as the Old Hand. The Au. has to ask the reader to accept his perception of the Old Hand as a man deeply embedded in the executive structure of the federal civil service. He can be thought of and likened to the power source of a nuclear submarine, closed off by the leaded walls of bureaucratic structure and cabinet committees, but at the same time, the derivative energy for arms of government over which he exerts no real control. His motive for seeking out the Au. — through an intermediary — is at this stage impossible to discern; there was only some vague reference to "historical truths." The Old Hand's style is rather ponderous but certainly not without courtesy or wit. He often prefaces a statement with "My information is . . .", or "It would seem that . . ." This does

117

not mean he is without opinion . . . "The Solicitor General? Yes, well perhaps the less said about him the better." The Au. has come away from their first meeting impressed with the depth of information and knowledge the Old Hand has of not only Security Service operations and officers, but also activities of foreign intelligence services in Canada.

He has unravelled for the Au. the question of what happened to the investigation initiated by DV and his desk officer, Wilson. It would seem that what ensued fully justified DV's growing cynicism. The Old Hand: "Wilson was very careful to keep the ambitious side of his nature from the other men. But his superior officers came to recognize that he was a real ass kisser. Wilson went to Letourneau, who was the Director General of Intelligence, with all the information that DV had put together without ever mentioning DV's role.

"I'm sure Letourneau probably had his own ideas about S, but Wilson's information — the CIA files and the long history of operational disasters — left Letourneau with the delicate problem of an internal investigation: how to put S under surveillance without his recognizing what was happening. He couldn't use the Watcher Service — they're all handpicked by S himself. The executive couldn't start excluding S from the flow of information for the simple reason that most of it came from him anyway, and any such action would tip S off that the game was up. Worst of all, Letourneau couldn't turn the problem over to Internal Security — S had organized that special branch. So Letourneau had to start from scratch. First of all he went to the other side and asked CO (Au: Criminal Operations) for four undercover narcotics agents from Vancouver.

Then he reached into the training college for some bright young recruits that nobody knew or could recognize. Then he pulled in a few more strange faces from the boondocks — men who were doing traffic duty in Coquitlam, B.C. In other words, he set up his own special security team. So far, so good, but the problem remained: how to put S under electronic surveillance. All the buggers were buddies of S — if you'll forgive the unintended pun.

"The solution was an outside contract. He hired a couple of experts that Major Copeland, the MI6 resident over in the British High Commission offices on Elgin St., flew in for him. Letourneau set up security for them one weekend and they installed a closed-circuit TV camera in the neon light receptacle over S's desk. Then Letourneau set up his new recruits in some forgotten storeroom where they spent hour after stupefied hour in front of two television sets.

"From what I've been told, the bottom third of the screen showed a slice of the top of S's head. The rest of the screen was taken up with whatever document S was reading or writing at the time. There was just one hitch to this plan. Letourneau had decided it would be smart to clear this secret investigation with the Commissioner. The Commissioner agreed, but on one condition — the camera was to be just enough out of focus so that the men watching would not be able to read the print on the documents. It was a classic Security Service operation. This particular group of men had been given special clearance to Top Secret for this high-level internal investigation, but the Commissioner was damned if he was going to let these constables read the same Top Secret documents he read.

Why? I rather imagine he found it too threatening to his own self-image.

"A bizarre situation, don't you think? The investigators were not allowed to read the documents even if this alleged double agent was absorbing it all and passing it, sentence by sentence, to the KGB. I don't know what they were supposed to do. I suppose the idea was that they might be able to catch him photocopying some document or furtively tucking material away in his briefcase, which, given his position, he had every right to do at the end of the day.

"Apparently this nonsense went on for about four months, with these men slowly losing their grip on sanity. Can you imagine what it would do to your morale, not to mention your mind, being forced to watch a blurred image on a television screen for eight to ten hours a day — given S's penchant for long working hours. Well, of course, the inevitable happened. The word got out and then some clown pinned a photograph on S's office door that blew the investigation wide open. A couple of years earlier, *Maclean's* magazine had run an article titled 'Our Man in Moscow' with a big blowup of Kim Philby walking across Red Square. This joker had cut out a small head shot of S, taken from an ancient issue of the RCMP staff magazine, and pasted it over Philby's face in the photograph.

"What did S do? He laughed. You would have thought it was the funniest thing he had seen in his life. He left the picture up there. Every morning he would come in, hesitate for a moment, look at the picture, chuckle, shake his head with a boys-will-be-boys kind of shrug and go to work. Letourneau was of course livid, but DV, I understand, almost ran amok when he discovered the stupid direction the investigation had taken without him. Wilson had meanwhile moved up the ladder, so DV went straight to Letourneau and told him what had originally happened. DV suggested there was nothing for it but to confront S and hope to break him down through lengthy and detailed interrogation. But Letourneau wanted to bug S's house, so the Brits were brought in again. What did they find out? That in his middle age, S was, in the vernacular, one hell of a stud. Let me tell you, there was shocked admiration in Letourneau's voice when he told the Commissioner: 'We don't know if this man's a double agent, but we do know he's one hell of a cocksmith.' Would you like to know what the Commissioner's reply was? 'This man lacks the moral character to be a member of the Force. Get rid of him.'

The Old Hand drained the dregs of his double Scotch and soda. "For me that remark was the clearest illustration of what happens when you have a southern Manitoba farmer, who happened to become a police-man, in ultimate charge of the nation's intelligence service. How did they finally get rid of S? Well, it wasn't that easy, and it took a considerable time, but if you'll excuse me, I'll go into that next time. I can see my driver has arrived to pick me up. Damned reliable chap, been with me for twelve years. Let me see, um-brella, briefcase. Right. Enjoyed our drink together. Next week, then? Excellent, bye, bye." And the Old Hand was gone in a wash of blue pinstripe.

* * * * *

"When I think of all the goddamned stunts that guy got us into . . ." DV is in a morose mood, his massive shoulders hunched pensively over the formica kitchen table in his bachelor highrise apartment. It is already ten-thirty on a weekday morning, and the Au. is surprised to find DV still unshaved, lingering over a cold cup of coffee, and obviously nursing a hangover. ("Bunch of hard drinkers stopped by last night.") In the bright morning sunlight the apartment looks even seedier, neglected. Ashtrays overflow with old cigarette butts. A couple of empty liquor bottles and some grimy glasses crowd the few available table-top spaces. The air is stale and heavy with the scent of leftover pizza pie.

The Au. is disturbed by his perception that the ordinarily brisk and conscientious DV is about to let go, beginning the slow drift to a limbo of booze, neglect, and the bitterness of unfulfilled ambition.

"That guy . . ." turns out to be S. Apparently DV and his drinking friends had been reliving old times in B Operations. "I have to tell you about Operation Boris — it became the catchword for a fouled-up operation. One afternoon this guy, who later turns out to be a minor clerk in the Defense Department phones the Soviet Embassy from an Ottawa pay phone. He tells the guy who answers the phone he wants to speak to somebody there who buys secrets. Not too swift, eh? The Russian is of course not interested. He knows that there are at least half a dozen taps on this phone call. So he more or less tells the clerk to get lost. But this guy is insistent, he tells the Russian to speak to somebody in authority, and to phone him back at this pay phone at five P.M. in two days' time. Sure enough, the clerk comes back to the same pay phone two days later and hangs around. And of course we're all there waiting for him. Nobody phones. So he phones the Soviet Embassy again, same story, nobody is interested. Beat it, they tell him. But anyway, the Watcher Service has now got a make on the guy and we check him out.

"As I said, he has this low-level job in the Defense Department. God knows what he intended to sell the Russians, drawings of fire extinguishers or some dumb thing like that. Well, we discover that this middle-aged, mild-mannered little clerk has got this torrid affair going with a good-looking babe of about thirty. Every lunch hour, when all the other peasants dive into their brown bags in the Defense Department basement cafeteria, he trundles down Elgin for a block or so and jumps into bed with his red-headed girlfriend. God knows what he's got, but whatever it is, she can't get enough of it.

"The guy is leading a double life. At five o'clock, he catches the bus to his wife and family. Every other weekend he spends in his playboy pad on Elgin or on trips to motels in Kingston — he has his wife convinced that he has to travel a lot for the department. This affair is the most exciting thing that has ever happened to him in his life, but it's very expensive. He pays for everything. And this is the guy's problem. He's got a double life, but only one job. He is behind in his mortgage payments, bills are piling up, but he doesn't want to turn out the lights on his affair. So from some magazine article, he gets the idea he can trick the Soviets into buying some phoney secrets.

"Normally we would just pick the guy up and tell him to cool it, but S has what is supposed to be this brilliant idea: 'We will run our own counter-deception operation. Somehow we're going to put this guy in touch with the Soviet Embassy, but the right way. Show him how to do it, and then feed him all kinds of crap that he in turn will feed them.

"Now here's the tricky part: we're going to accomplish all this without his ever knowing the Security Services is manipulating the scene, at least in the beginning. So, stage one: We contact him as the KGB. I phone down to translation services. 'Send me up a guy with a big Slavic face and a heavy Russian accent.' Yeah, it's just like central casting. They send up Boris; blond, about five foot, built like a fireplug, and with an accent right off the Nevsky Prospect. Perfect! We even find him a big floppy fedora and a trench coat. 'Okay, Boris,' I coach him, 'this is all you have to do. See this guy in the photograph. Every day at one minute after twelve he rushes out of the Defense Department and down Elgin St. You are going to stop him, and what are you going to say?'

" 'Hello, I am Boris, they send for me for the informations.'

" 'Excellent! and then you slip this envelope into his hand, and say only one more sentence . . .'

" 'Sure, I know, I know . . . Follow instruction. Vee meet next wik.'

"Everything is perfect, the Russian accent is right out of a Grade B movie. The only problem is he keeps nipping on a bottle. What's the matter? I ask him. 'It's notting, notting, jus'a nervous,' he tells me. 'Okay, let's go through it again.' I remember that I thought then I should find another Boris — but, no time.

"Lunch hour comes along. Boris grabs the clerk's sleeve at the right moment: 'Hello, I am Boris . . .'

124

Well, it just floors this guy from the Defense Department. He can't get over it. 'My god,' he whispers, 'what an organization' — we have Boris all wired up for sound — he rips open the envelope right there on the street. There's two hundred and fifty dollars in it and a sheet of instructions for the next meeting. The clerk is really excited now. He peers up and down the street. All the time he won't let go of Boris's arm. 'Listen, buddy, I mean Boris, we have to talk.' And he drags him into the nearest bar. They stay in the bar the whole lunch hour. Then they have a few more drinks, and buy a couple for the cocktail waitress. They find out they like each other, they keep drinking. Finally it's five o'clock. Boris is awfully pissed. He leans over to tell the clerk, 'Lissen, I like. You have for to unnerstand Boris is no a spy. Work for RCMP. Bes' dam' job Boris ever had.' When the clerk finally gets the message, they both start laughing like hell and wind up spending the rest of the evening in the pub. Operation Boris.''

Half-an-hour later the Au. is ready to doubt his earlier perception of DV's depression. Because shaved, dressed in a lightweight suit, and driving downtown, DV once again gives off that quality of powerful confidence that so marks his physical presence. (It will be three weeks later that the Au. discovers the drinking party marked DV's final decision to resign from the Force.) Turning his inconspicuous Chevy Nova down Bronson Ave., DV gives a grunt of professional interest. The Au. has the impression that DV's street antenna had been turned on to full alert.

"Want to know something? We're right in the middle of a Watcher Service operation. See that goofy looking little guy running like hell down the side street on our right? If you could follow him all the way you would see him diving into the back seat of a big black Ford that's already moving and in which another guy is holding the back door open for him. My guess is that the target vehicle is that blue Buick about three cars ahead of us. Yeah, that's it. You see all the action is going on along the two streets on either side of this one, so the guy who is being followed is never under the impression that somebody's tailing him. All the men and women from the Watcher Service are in radio contact. The tailing cars operate on the parallel streets. The watchers are dropped off at street corners ahead of the car. They have small but powerful walkie-talkies so they run like hell to the anticipated intersection, check the car under surveillance through the intersection, then barrel back down the side street to the pickup vehicle which will then leapfrog him to the next point. Yeah, you're right, you've got to be in shape for that kind of intelligence work. Those guys really have to move it. How do they operate on a highway? It's a little more complex. Can involve anything up to a dozen cars. But I'll tell you, if you ever think you're being followed on the highway, go like hell and then just over the crest of the first hill, pull over fast, run around and throw up the hood — pretend you have engine trouble. Take down the plate numbers of the first five or six cars that come over the hill. Five miles further down the road, repeat the performance. If you come up with two or three same numbers — you know you're it.

"You have to hand it to S, he put together a crack unit, and that's where he impressed the hell out of the cavalry officers. The question remains though: to what use is all this technique being applied? What do you say we hang in and find out? You will have an un- equalled opportunity, a theoretical and practical dem- onstration of the RCMP's Watcher Service. Ah, hah. He's turned into the garage of the Skyline Hotel. Well, we'll just park on a meter and walk in. It looks to me as if they were expecting him, because they've got a whole reception committee.'' Loitering outside the main entrance to the hotel the Au. recognizes the same Indian panhandler who had accosted DV on the Canal. Only this time when DV reaches into his pocket for some change, he asks, ''Where's the action?''

''On the roof, the restaurant,'' comes the instant reply. ''Let's give them a few minutes,'' says DV and he steers the Au. into a ground-floor bar, where they spend ten minutes over a few sips of beer, before tak- ing the elevator to the rooftop restaurant of the Skyline Hotel. The restaurant is almost empty. A woman who looks as though she could be an employee of the hotel sits in a chair, chatting to the checkroom attendant. DV leads the way to a table far from the few seated diners. ''Well, there are the two stars of the show. The Latin- looking gentleman over there on the far side is the sec- ond secretary from the Cuban Embassy. I rather think that's who was driving the rented Buick we happened on back there on Bronson. The man opposite him with his nose in the menu you probably know.'' Indeed, the Au. vaguely recognizes one of those earnest young journalists who scrape out a living working for small- circulation left-wing magazines. ''They must have used this place before, because they have everybody waiting for them. The nice old gent at the next table gazing idly at the view is from the Watcher Service and is wired for sound and is recording their conversation. The bus-boy in the white jacket is a Spanish-speaking Watcher who, should the two men wander over to the buffet, will very helpfully hover at their shoulders. The mousy-looking brunette talking to the checkroom attendant will notify the guys waiting downstairs if there is a sudden unanticipated departure from the restaurant. This is high-level surveillance. Expensive as hell, it has probably tied up forty or fifty people for the day. But whatever those two guys over there are talking about, you and I will never know. Maybe the guys on the Cuban desk will tell me. But if my experience means anything, the Canadian taxpayer is probably paying a hundred thousand bucks to find out that our journalist friend over there wants a two-week freebie to Cuba for himself and his girlfriend. But I guess that's the nature of the beast. What do I mean? Well, like just about every other department in Security Services, the Watcher Service has become an institution. And if you create an institution then you have to keep feeding the monster so that it can stay alive — at least that's how the bureaucrats who run this organization operate. Well now, look at this!'' Krista Gollner has just entered the restaurant, and, on catching sight of the Cuban and his lunch guest, joins them at their table.

SECTION VI

For the first time the Au. is not in a position of starting cold with a source. The Lawyer S has hired, the "heads-up, today kind of person" is actually a young man the Au. has known for some time. There is even a distant family connection: a first cousin once removed married to a nephew.

The Au. remembers the wedding: a stifling Don Mills affair of the *nouveau riche*. The older generation of plumbing contractors and real estate developers faced with the hostility of their offspring: budding lawyers, doctors, architects — the emerging mercenaries of the upper-middle class. A tacit truce had been called for the day of the wedding, broken here and there in minor brush fires when the testiness of age and the arrogance of spoiled youth grated unbearably across the truce lines. But these were quickly extinguished as the tribe of three hundred guests basked in the reflected ritual of a formal wedding. The derived satisfaction must have been shortlived. Three years later, the couple had parted. He to bury himself in a Bay St. stockbrokerage house. She to win some small degree of notoriety as the star of underground pornographic films made in the US.

The Lawyer is a slight man, almost slender. His open choirboy's face and a diffident soft-spoken manner are nevertheless the vehicle for a quick and aggressive intelligence. It is the kind of personality which tends to disarm his colleagues and judges. And perhaps pushes him to certain *macho* forms of compensation: For example, he rides a 750 c.c. Ducati, an enormously large and loud motorcycle, on which he thunders around Toronto in the pursuit of his legal practice.

Although totally different in manner, he shares with the EA the same irreverence for the mystique which has grown up and surrounds many of society's institutions. His answer to a tentative request by the Au. to discuss as "background information" the circumstances surrounding the secret inquiry into S's role in Security Services for the past twenty years elicited a cheerful: "I wouldn't have gone out of my way to approach you about it, but seeing that you have contacted me I would be happy to talk to you any time." And it was on that unexpected and easy agreement the Au. met with the Lawyer in his temporary Ottawa base, a suite of luxurious rooms in the Carleton Towers hotel. For although he might be a radical lawyer, he has at the same time found his radicalism extremely successful, and is much sought after.

Newspapers and files cluttered the long spacious couch. A motorcycle jacket and helmet had been tossed into an armchair. The Lawyer wore an open blue silk shirt revealing a white pukka necklace against a sun-tanned throat. Worn blue jeans tucked into scuffed leather jackboots completed the ensemble. The Au. half-expected to find the Ducati propped under the glass chandelier in the bedroom, leaking tiny drops of oil onto the ornate broadloom.

The Lawyer made room for the Au. on the couch by moving aside a framed and intricately wrought piece of *petit point* which carried the delicately embroidered words, *Sue the Bastards*. "A gift from an admirer," chuckled the Lawyer, "I thought that when all this is over I can pass it on to S. No, it has nothing to do with whether or not I think he is guilty. I just can't see how they're ever going to prove anything. The inquiry has been going for a week now and all that has come out so far has been a great deal of evidence about RCMP bungling and incompetence. I gather the point they're trying to make is that my client is responsible for a long series of operational flops and therefore a double agent of some kind. But so far, there isn't anything that would stand up in court.

"My client's attitude? It is one of total cooperation. I must say he is quite a remarkable guy. All the RCMP officers are giving evidence from reams of files and notes. He just sits there, listening quietly, and then from memory adds a great deal of detail that has been left out, but the addition of which subtly shifts all this circumstantial guilt away from himself and on to the shoulders of the officers giving evidence. I have the feeling that he really doesn't need me at all. No, I'm certainly not bored. I find it all quite fascinating.

"Your friend DV was presenting evidence yesterday and today. He went over a couple of cases he worked on while he was an investigator on the Czech desk in B Operations. The first one involved a Czech military attaché who had held several secret meetings with a Czech lawyer here called Woytek. After six months of surveillance and on S's orders, DV intercepted Woytek in the middle of the Pointe Claire bridge in Montreal, drove him to a Montreal hotel room where, after about twenty-four hours of interrogation, it seemed that Woytek was about to make a deal. He was apparently going to offer his services as a double agent or just tell everything he knew about the Czech STB. But first he wanted to have some guarantee of immunity from prosecution. S couldn't give that guarantee. This was before they had a DGI. An Assistant Commissioner, in this case Smellie, was in overall charge of Security Services. Smellie was adamant: 'No deals, arrest the bastard and bring him in.' So they booked him and they spent two weeks interrogating him, tore his house apart, his office files, everything, and they got absolutely nothing.

"I could see the point DV was trying to make. He was suggesting that S knew what Smellie's reaction would be. And that by picking up Woytek at that time and making sure he didn't get immunity, he blocked what might have been an effective penetration of the Czech intelligence service. But that point was quickly squashed by the Red Tory (Au: Red Tory? One of the three members of parliament sitting on the panel of inquiry.) who asked: 'Do you mean to suggest that an RCMP superintendent should be in the position to waive criminal prosecution and grant a traitor immunity?' and when DV replied: 'Within the context of intelligence gathering, yes,' all three members of parliament simply shook their heads with a 'Good God, what a simpleton' attitude. But I'm afraid they did take DV more seriously today when he presented evidence in what they describe as the 'Sgt. Blake affair.'

132

"Yes, it's even more interesting than the Woytek case. DV had apparently spent about nine months developing a contact with another Czech officer and had already got him 'turned around' when S suddenly assigned this Sgt. Blake as DV's backup man to the case. I must say your friend DV is explicit. He described Sgt. Blake as 'a total fuckup.' Blake had all kinds of problems. He was over his head in debt. He was separated from his wife, and had got one of the stenos at headquarters pregnant. According to DV, he had fought hard with S to get Blake taken off the assignment. But S insisted, saying the man had the makings of a good intelligence officer. That he needed a challenge and a solid intelligence project to get his teeth into and take his mind off his problems. Under orders, DV tolerated Blake for a couple of months. The situation resolved itself when Blake suddenly resigned from the Force. Somehow he had found some financial backing to set up a marina in the Georgian Bay tourist area. About two months later, DV's double agent was temporarily reassigned by the STB to Prague for special courses in micro-dot techniques. Unfortunately the Czech just disappeared without a trace a few minutes after he landed in Prague.

"At this point in the evidence, and I can tell you everyone was quite glued to their seats, totally intrigued by the story, DV produced a file which he described as 'from an allied intelligence service' and that (for security reasons which he could not go into) had not been passed on to the RCMP until four years later.

"This file revealed that Blake had betrayed the double agent for fifty thousand dollars, and had been observed by agents of the 'friendly intelligence service' receiving the payoff in an Ottawa supermarket. DV then went on to insist that S had known all along that Blake was extremely vulnerable and purposely put him in the position where he could be approached and bribed by a KGB agent working out of the Soviet Embassy. In other words, S set Blake up.

"The Red Tory then asked DV if he could prove what he had described as 'his conclusions.' DV blew his cool. He started shouting: 'What further proof do you want, a smoking pistol? Do you want the bugged conversation of S setting it up? Do you want a photograph of him talking it over with the KGB resident? Because if you do, you'll never get it, because that's not how it's done.' He was quite beside himself at this point; I got the impression of a man on his way to cracking up. Unfortunately for S, it also creates a strong impression of a sincere man strongly exercised. 'Well, how is it done?' asked one of the MPs. DV was quite blunt: 'If I knew, sir, we wouldn't be going through this farce.' At that point they called an adjournment for the day."

* * * * *

It would be of no great advantage to the reader for the Au. to describe at any length the fencing match he played with Atkinson, when they finally met for a drink — that is, after the Au. had twice postponed their appointment.

The Au. had thought to divert Atkinson's curiosity by giving him the story of how the president of Spearhead Industries had been able to stave off for so long

RCMP prosecution for his fraudulent financial activities: One evening a member of H Operations approached the doorman of the posh condominium in which the president of Spearhead, John Loyal, owned the ninth floor. An intelligence officer from H had tucked a hundred-dollar bill into the doorman's hand, and told him there would be more if he would let the officer know the next time Loyal left town. The doorman, being nobody's fool, immediately told Loyal what had happened. The president thanked the doorman with another hundred dollars and told him exactly when he was leaving town. The next Thursday, Loyal, accompanied by his male secretary, drove out to his Lear jet at Uplands airport. The secretary boarded the plane, which took off for Vancouver, and Loyal returned to his secretary's apartment where he stayed until one in the morning. Then, with his lawyer, he returned to his own ninth-floor apartment. Where, surprise! they discovered several officers from H Branch and fifteen men from E Branch busy drilling holes into the ceilings.

The red-faced SS officers explained that they were not so much interested in Loyal — Criminal Operation already had the goods on him — as in his neighbors on the tenth floor, who just happened to be the delegation from the People's Republic of China, and that these holes were for the purpose of installing sensitive listening devices into the floors.

Loyal sympathized with the problem. And said, being a "patriotic Canadian," he would certainly agree to the installation of the bugs in what was *his* ceiling on the condition that he first be given back his passport — it had been taken away from him three months earlier when RCMP officers from Criminal Operations first laid charges. And, second, that the RCMP delay the prosecution of charges against him for the next two years. All right, agreed the RCMP, rather churlishly. Although there was a moment of high humor in the subsequent court proceedings when the RCMP lawyer accepted with a straight face Loyal's request for the return of his passport: His doctor had ordered him "for the sake of his health to ski that winter in the Swiss Alps."

Atkinson liked the story and thanked the Au., saying he might be able to use it sometime. But then continued to ply the Au. with many drinks and to press hard for information about his investigation of S. The Au. fenced and smiled, never sure of whether Atkinson was acting out of his own curiosity or in the interests of the RCMP whom he served so well.

But just before they rose to part, Atkinson surprised the Au. by stating quite vehemently: "Listen, you should forget DV. He is only a bit player in all this. He is also a man obsessed. An officer like that can no longer see the spy business as a game. He degrades and corrupts the game, much in the same way as professional hockey players who have lost their sense of fun and play and have reduced the game of hockey to work. Forget DV. You have to get past the DVs in this business. Believe me, you have to understand one important fact: the CIA is manipulating, yes, running this whole show. That's first and last. Now repeat after me: 'The CIA is manipulating this show.' He chanted the words in a singsong, waving his hands in time as if teaching a kindergarten class a new song. Then Atkinson unexpectedly grew serious again. "Listen, I'm going to give it to you. Give you the *key*. Not because I like you. Not because you helped me years ago when I was naked and a stranger. Not because you can do this better than a straight journalist. But simply because I know my TV network will not handle it. They're scared of the libel, scared of what it might do, scared that it might bring their whole profit structure tumbling down. So, me, Terry Atkinson, is going to give you the key: it's Krista Gollner, S's former lover. You have to find some way to get close to her. And now I have to go, because drunk as I am, 'I have . . . what is it? . . . miles to go, and promises to keep, before I lay me down to sleep.' Doesn't sound quite right, but that's the drift. Goodnight and good luck.''

* * * * *

"Hey, d'ya read the *New York Times*?'' It is the Executive Assistant to the Solicitor General on the phone. His tone carries an undercurrent of excitement that slurs his usually precise diction. ''There's something there on page seven that I think will interest you. Yeah, remember my telling you about that strange party down in Washington that I went to with the SG, the one with all the weird intelligence creeps, and there was this tall skinny guy who spilled the beans about S being interrogated by the CIA . . . you remember, eh? Right, well, the skinny guy is right there on page seven, only he's dead. He was found in a Houston motel room trussed up like a turkey and wired up to the electrical outlet; a painful way to go, I understand. His wife says it was murder. The cops say it was suicide. How come the police, with all their experience, always have the most unbelievable explanations? Anyway, his wife says his job was to feed misleading information to the Soviets. Someone here on the Soviet desk says the method is a KGB trademark. It's the way they deal with people who have double-crossed them. But his wife claims that her husband had found out something that he shouldn't have and that the CIA bumped him off and made it look like a KGB job. Who the hell can you believe, anyway? Freaky, eh? Yeah, right, today's paper, page seven. That's okay, thought you might be interested. Right, have a nice day.''

* * * * *

"Ah, shit on the RCMP." It is DV's wife speaking and she is not at all the kind of person the Au. imagined. A short shapeless body, and behind a round sour face — and, yes, a truly "venemous breath" — an intelligence that is alert and perceptive. But, she is devoid of human social skills, although, strangely enough, her job description is "human engineer" in some hidden valley of the civil service landscape, or more precisely the computer service division of Supply and Services of the federal government. In a monosyllabic — at least on her part — telephone conversation she reluctantly agreed to meet with the Au. on this Friday afternoon for "A cup of coffee at Nate's on the Sparks Street Mall." The interview is not going well.

The Au. had at first found DV's wife unexpectedly prickly and hostile. She seemed concerned that the Au. was embarked on an enterprise that would be "just one more puff glorifying the RCMP's role." Now she reveals her bitterness and is constantly at the point of

138

preoccupied desperation about him. I could feel it even in his lovemaking; a kind of desperate abandon that verged on wild joy. I think it's the way men behave when they recognize they are out of their depth and their life no longer has any recognizable reference points. But then women are the same — and one has to have some safety outlets, I suppose. After that, things went just dead between us. Perhaps he realized that there was nothing he was ever really going to be able to do about S. I think he could no longer bring himself to believe in what they call "the game", and the spirit of play seemed to go out of his own life.

"But then what alternative did he have? Leave the RCMP and start his own security firm? That's just another word for strikebusting and DV has always had too much respect for working people to make money from that kind of filth. Not that it ever became a serious issue, because no matter how badly he was treated, he retained an almost mystic faith in the RCMP. It became another wedge between us. I came to the conclusion that intellectually I am far tougher and more radical than he is. From then on it was just a slow drifting apart. What are the things that make you finally leave someone? You can no longer deal with the trivial annoyances: the way he used to slurp sliced oranges after he came in from one of his runs along the canal bank. But I don't want to remember that time now — I'm not very proud of the way I behaved. There are other men now, other lovers. And I suppose I am a little weepy because it is the end of what has been a tough week, and over the remembrance of things past. What do I think about S? Frankly, I couldn't give a goddamn about S, or anything else about the RCMP. Excuse me, I have to go.'' And abruptly, sniffling into a Kleenex, she stands up and hurriedly threads her way through the crowded tables, ignoring the curious stares of the office workers on their afternoon coffee breaks.

* * * * *

A tall blond man with an athletic build strides briskly across the park. He is dressed in an expensive pinstripe charcoal suit, alligator shoes, and has a copy of the German newspaper, *Frankfurter Allgemeine* folded under one arm. Without a glance for the other occupant of the park bench, he sits down and begins to read his newspaper. "Herr Kling?"

The introduction over, Kling graciously accepts the compliments on his health, particularly, as the Au. points out, he is supposed to have been dead for almost two years. Would Herr Kling like to comment on the circumstances surrounding his "death" and his resurrection? "Thank you, but I would rather not discuss such matters. After all, I have now established my headquarters in the Far East. I am only passing through, a temporary guest, so to speak, in Canada; therefore I wouldn't wish to embarrass the Canadian government in any way. I'm afraid it is only possible for me to talk about those events which preceeded my, uh . . . departure.'' Kling speaks with a soft mellow voice that is so persuasive in its sincerity it is almost as though he is able to wrap his words, touched with a light German accent, into a fine envelope of plausability. The Au. is also struck by Kling's likeness to the man he glimpsed a few days ago in Krista's bed. But he cannot be sure. The man in the bed was lying with his face turned toward the window, and the Au. had only a momentary foreshortened view of one side of his face. And yet . . .

"Yes, I knew S. I had dinner with him on several occasions. A delightful man. He has that . . . I don't know the English word for it, and in German we use the French cliché savoir-faire. It is a quality I miss so much in North America. It seems that most often it is the Europeans that you meet in this part of the world who are the only ones to have that attractive depth, the curious mind. Do you know what I mean? Well, certainly S has it. Yes, a most attractive man. It distresses me a great deal to hear about his current problems. I only wish that I could be of some assistance. He was very helpful to me. I think that he was probably the only person in the RCMP Security Services who understood my problems with the Mossad — you know who they are? Exactly, Israeli intelligence. Enormously powerful organization. They hounded me from one country to another with all these outrageous stories that I was an arms dealer, that I supplied the Arab terrorists with weapons, that I myself assassinated a police detective in Milan. A man whom I had never met and whom I had killed as a favor to a group of anarchists. How ridiculous! I mean, look at me — do I look like an anarchist, a terrorist?

"I will tell you the truth of what happened. It is simply this: My father was a successful businessman in the oil industry, and with great courage and superior moral conviction took it upon himself to hold the interests of several international oil companies under his, shall we say, *stewardship* during the Nazi regime. After the war

142

he restored these assets to their rightful owners. In long court proceedings, conducted by the allied governments, he was cleared of any wrongdoing and the baseless accusations of using slave labor that were brought against him by certain individuals. Let me tell you," and here Kling leans forward to tap the Au.'s knee with an emphatic forefinger, "there are still many extremely important oilmen in America today who are very grateful for my father's responsible behavior during the war years. Unfortunately, there are many people who absolutely refused to recognize the court's decisions. So when I followed in my father's footsteps and became an oilman, and enjoyed some degree of success in the Middle East, these same people, no longer able to attack my father, decided to destroy me. And this is the reason I was finally driven out of the Middle East, Italy, and even my own country. If I may say so, it has all the elements of a Greek tragedy: A man driven from his country to live in exile by demons powerless against an honorable father. I believed that Canada offered me a new promise, a new start in life. I still believe that it is one of the few places in the world that a young man can put together a fortune unhampered by the restrictions and heavy taxes that exist in other countries. It was in this spirit of trust and ambition that I came here. Unfortunately my enemies in the Mossad pursued me across the Atlantic. I do not think Canadians comprehend how widely based and how powerful an organization it is. Did you know that one of the Mossad death squads, the group who in October of 1972 murdered an innocent Palestinian in Norway, were travelling on Canadian passports? Yes, my friend, legal Canadian passports, obtained through

Canadian aircraft carrier, the HMCS Bonaventure, which had been refitted eighteen months earlier for a price of close to eighteen million dollars, had been sold for scrap at seven hundred and fifty thousand. The Bonnie, as I understand Canadians affectionately called her, was at that time being towed from Halifax harbor by a Japanese deep-sea tug. The destination was a scrapyard in Taiwan.

"After some consultation with my business associates in the Middle East, I learned that the Indian navy owned the sister carrier to the Bonaventure — they were both built in British shipyards during the last year of the war. The Indian ship had never been refitted and the Indian defense department was keen to do business. One of my business associates caught up with the tug and the Bonaventure in Capetown, where they had stopped for refuelling and minor repairs. From there it was a fairly simple matter for them to rendezvous with a group of vessels of the Indian navy on exercises in the Indian Ocean. I myself flew out there. We entertained the tug's crew with food, wine and some of the most beautiful whores I could find and bring out from Bombay for this three-day party at sea. After it was all over, the tub sailed off with a carrier on its tow line, and the Indian navy had acquired a refitted aircraft carrier at a considerable saving. No, I am not free to divulge the figures involved. But I can tell you that after I had paid everyone, my margin was not much more than a million and a half dollars. Not the biggest deal I have made but certainly worth the effort involved. I beg your pardon? No. It would be a betrayal of a gentleman's trust to reveal the amounts I paid to the other parties involved.

"Yes, I did meet S once again after that, we had a pleasant dinner together. It was at his suggestion that I did my, ah . . . disappearing act — a truly brilliant idea. Don't you think? Now, if you'll excuse me, I am leaving for San Francisco this evening and I have several small matters to clear up. No, I'm not worried that you will reveal me to the authorities. In the first place your discretion is guaranteed by people I trust. Secondly, who on earth is going to believe that you could bring a man back from the dead? Third, I surely must have friends in high places. *Auf Wiedersehen.*"

* * * * *

DV will not talk to the Au. about his appearances before the three-man board of inquiry; even pretends not to know what the Au. is talking about. And in a not very adroit attempt to divert the Au.'s line of questioning, points to a newspaper story on the front page of his morning newspaper: "Goddam reporters," he growls, "over the last few weeks this guy has created The Stabber, simply by pulling together six unsolved killings that have happened over the last four months. He has half the women of Ottawa terrified. It's all the stenos at headquarters can talk about. Listen to this: 'Posters of police sketches on the walls of the University ask for information that will lead to the arrest of a knife-wielding, long-haired young man wanted for several attacks on female students . . . blah, blah, blah . . . However, Inspector of Detectives, J. Langlois refused to comment on the possibility that the body of the elderly priest found stabbed to death under the Bronson Bridge at 4 A.M. this morning has any con-

146

nection with the five earlier murders in the vicinity of the canal, or the suspect portrayed in the posters' . . . For Chrissakes!'' DV tosses the newspaper in the general direction of his wastepaper basket. ''All that guy is doing is creating hysteria.'' DV invites the Au. to bring his coffee out onto the balcony of his apartment. ''Might as well enjoy the last of the fine weather. Seems like there's already a bit of a nip in the air. In a few days time we're going to wake up and find all that goddamn white stuff over everything.''

They stand sipping their coffee in silence, judges in a concrete box, surveying the autumnal landscape. The trees are almost bereft of leaves. The grass has turned a dark yellow. Buildings previously hidden by the summer's foliage, are now discernible. The additional depth of vision reveals squat concrete buildings, and gives the Au. the feeling that the city itself is hunkering down in apprehension of the approaching long months of winter. ''You know,'' said DV addressing the cool morning air, ''I could never figure those CIA bastards out. When I sat in on all those interrogations of S, I found it hard to believe that son-of-a-bitch Daniels was doing anything more than going through the motions.''

SECTION VII

It has become a regular evening ritual for the Au. to drop in on the Lawyer and, over a glass of dry vermouth on the rocks, catch up on the events of the day at the special inquiry into S's activities.

The Lawyer: "I'm afraid the picture is looking more serious for S. It's not so much that any hard proof has yet been offered. It's just the sheer staggering weight of circumstantial evidence that's mounting against him. I must say, though, that he remains quite cool in the face of it all. From our discussions, I'm sure that he must be sensitive to what is going on. I certainly feel it. There's been a definite switch in the attitude of the three members of parliament. The Red Tory keeps wanting to come back to the Sgt. Blake incident. Today he asked that DV be brought back to answer more questions about Blake. There *are* a lot of interesting questions: Why wasn't Blake prosecuted after the information about his payoff was received from the 'friendly intelligence service'? — which we all take to be the CIA. What were the reasons for the three-year delay in passing the information to the RCMP? The NDP member even wants to call the two intelligence officers who witnessed the payoff before the court. Fat chance.

"Yes, I've discussed this turn of events with S, and he doesn't seem unduly concerned. I dunno, but I've sat beside enough cool customers like him before not to realize that he has something up his sleeve. I hope he talks it over with me before deciding to drop some sort of bombshell on the proceedings. Situations like that tend to age lawyers unnecessarily.

"But what I really wanted to talk to you about was what they did to him when all this started. I didn't think that I could be shocked by anything any more — disgusted, yes, but not shocked — yet I certainly was today. He told me that the day after he was first brought back from Australia, they took him over to a special section in the National Research Council building, and there they gave him what they call the Belfast Treatment, which turns out to be a misnomer because from what S tells me, this special form of torture was devised and developed under a defense contract by the white-coated gnomes of our own National Research Council laboratories.

"They put him in a special soundproof, floodlit cell, completely bare. Then for twenty-four hours he was subjected to a barrage of sound, continual tape recordings at about ninety decibels, which hovers around the pain threshold. (Au: Irreparable cell damage begins at about a hundred and eighteen decibels.) No, it wasn't music: the noise of jet engines, heavy industrial equipment grinding away, high-pitched whines of drills. That sort of highly aggravating sound. Sometimes separately, sometimes all mixed together. Then they would give him absolute silence in total darkness for twelve hours; a 'desensitizing cell' they called it. Then he would get another twenty-four hours of the blasting sound treatment with the room illuminated in stark white light. Apparently this went on for about five or six days. After which he was interrogated continuously for another two days.

"Certainly I told him we must present this information to the members of the inquiry! But he won't let me, because he still has this curious 'sense of loyalty to the force.' And he claims the RCMP doesn't even know about the facilities at the NRC. And that the whole interrogation was run by 'those military intelligence thugs' as he calls them. I asked if they had got anything out of him during the interrogation that was . . . well, damaging; and that as his lawyer I should know about. He gave me an amused look and said simply: 'Of course not.'

"We then got into a discussion of how sophisticated systems of torture have become. He told me this incredible story about a group of Brazilian and Argentinian doctors who came up to the Johns Hopkins University Hospital in Maryland to learn all the most advanced plastic surgery techniques. Then they went back to their home countries to carry out these truly frightening operations on their own people.

"No, not really as experiments, but as medical technology used to control the population. Because the military and secret police in Argentina were having a difficult time capturing the leaders of the revolutionary groups such as the ERP and the Monteneros, they would capture their wives or girlfriends. It seems that a favorite was to take one of these women, pull all her teeth, and then, through plastic surgery, remove most of her lips and reduce her mouth to a small O — so that she would at least be able to feed herself with a straw. But during the surgery and postoperative period, she would receive the best of care: intravenous feeding so there was no weight loss, even sun lamps. So that when the flesh had completely healed, she was still in the best of physical health; but her mental health — God knows what nightmarish damage had been done to her mind. The final act was to take her in an unmarked police car, with a light scarf around her face, then release her into her old neighborhood. All her friends and family would rush up to greet her and embrace, and then be confronted with this monster that these so-called physicians had created.

"What happened to them? S told me that the fortunate ones got out through the auspices of the Swedish Embassy. They are now in Cuba and the Soviet Union where doctors are trying to put them back together — at least physically. I don't know that there is any mental treatment that could make a person who had been subjected to that agony ever feel whole again."

* * * * *

The thick brown envelope is fourteen by eight inches. It is the double-lined and padded type that is used to protect books or tapes during shipment. There is no address, simply the Au.'s name written large in sprawling blue-inked letters. Certainly nothing to indicate who sent the envelope, which the Au. found ten minutes ago in his mailbox.

What do you do with an unexpected package that arrives in such anonymous fashion? If you are the Au. you stare at it for long paranoid minutes before coming to the belated realization that if an unknown enemy wanted to send a booby-trapped envelope, it would surely be less suspicious-looking. The address would be typewritten, there would be postage, or at least a uniformed delivery service. On the basis of this tenuous logic, the Au. reaches forward and in one "well, here goes" movement rips open the envelope, and immediately feels more than a little foolish. Because what spills out on the table is a bundle of letters, still in their original envelopes held together with a wide elastic band, and a small cardboard folder containing two lengthy newspaper clippings. Last, a photograph that the Au. immediately recognizes: He once again finds himself peering at a hostile young woman in a loose jellaba squinting against the glare of light in a sun-drenched Arab courtyard.

Carefully — for some irrational reason the Au. half-expects the letters to disintegrate between his fingers — he loosens them from their rubber band and withdraws them from their envelopes. He is surprised (and also a little embarrassed) to find that they are loveletters to Krista. They are unsigned and written on a typewriter. Are they from S? But why a typewriter? Is it because he had no confidence in Krista's ability to decipher his notorious scrawl? The first letter contains references to Krista's departure, and then the dreams the letter-writer has of following her along the canal path while Krista was "arm-in-arm with another man." The other letters were presumably written before she had left and are full of great tenderness and enigmatic references to what can only be surmised as shared moments of passion and sensual delight. (What was it Krista had told the Au. about S's passion? Ah, yes. "For him sex was a celebration of the flesh.") Aside from these emotions, the letters are quite banal in their content, but then other people's loveletters probably always are. The last envelope holds a note from Krista. It is clearly addressed to S; a short, surprisingly self-pitying note informing him that she is leaving. The note, although well-phrased, carries the uncomfortable ring of emotionally immature manipulation.

The newspaper clippings are more interesting. They are from the Washington *Post* and the New York *Times,* photocopies of the originals. The subject of the news stories is a former citizen of the Soviet Union, Yuri Nosenko, who, according to the *Post* story, had been a high official of the KGB's North American section, and who had defected from East Berlin (exactly how was not revealed) to members of the CIA in West Berlin some months after the assassination of John Kennedy in 1963.

Nosenko was apparently kept in secret confinement for the next four years, ostensibly for fear that he would be assassinated by KGB agents, but more probably to learn whether he was intended as a plant — an agent carrying information and documents of misleading and deceiving material.

The New York *Times* story carried, in essence, the same information with a few additional paragraphs that had been circled in red ink. The first paragraph reported:

Nosenko had brought with him, according to undisclosed sources, the codes and cover names of the individuals who formed the support structures for KGB spying and government infiltration operations in North America.

153

The newspaper stories were datelined September 1968. So that meant Nosenko had been kept under wraps for something like five years. (The FBI had supplied Nosenko with "a new alias and history" that would allow him to spend the rest of his life in peaceful anonymity in some corner of the US.)

The subsequent encircled paragraphs went on to surmise that once Nosenko had furnished the authorities with the information, the CIA and the FBI were confronted with a multiple problem: first, how to track down and identify the coded spies; next, once they were identified, should they be fed false information that would then be funnelled back to the Soviet Union? or should an attempt be made to turn them around and make them double agents? The reporter, who obviously had a background in intelligence, concluded with the thought that the only reason the Nosenko story had been leaked was because of the failure or success of the counter-intelligence agencies in North America with Nosenko's information.

The Au. is unable to control or break the repetitive cycle of his mind as he reads and rereads the zeroxed newspaper clipping, his eyes racing over the print. He can feel that recognizable surge of excitement that comes with the "special find" — "the real thing;" and which follows weeks and months of work, research, and interviews. The newsclippings had provoked the startling realization: If S had been among the spies "blown" by Nosenko, then the CIA had known, possibly as far back as 1964, that S was a KGB agent, and had obviously never informed the RCMP.

SECTION VIII

The Old Hand's thick fleshy fingers wrap themselves around the cut-glass tumbler of whisky. Corded purple veins swell ominously under the thin skin of the back of his hand, probe whorls of close grey hair, then wind rope-like along a heavily boned wrist to finally disappear under an immaculate white cuff held together with a burnished gold cufflink.

The Au. is uncomfortable. The Old Hand is too much at ease in this dark oak-panelled study with its low flickering log fire in the grate. There is too much power in this room. The Au. is disturbed by the thought that he is not here as an invited guest, but rather has been ushered into "a presence," to be first patronized and then manipulated. Perhaps he is being unfair, his normal perceptions stifled by the oppressive atmosphere of self-recognition that is so dominant in the room. He feels hypnotized by the Old Hand's baronial manner of speech and deep gravelly voice, and recognizes that this is the voice of a man who has known power and privilege all his life, and seems never to have questioned that it should be any other way.

At the same time the Au. has come to see the Old Hand as a Cimmerian figure, a man who has made his deals with life in the murk of the dark, perpetual night of the soul — that his power has come from his decision to know men and women only by their vulnerabilities and weaknesses. As if sensing the Au.'s thoughts, the Old Man muses aloud: "You know, we will never know how many voices of dissent the Security Services has been able to silence.

"No, no, this is no Gulag." (An impatient wave of his hand.) "We have a far more subtle method of dealing with people who raise too many questions. In a capitalist society money is oxygen, without money you can't breathe. Threaten a man with the loss of employment or take away his credit and you threaten him with suffocation. We are a society in which people are defined by what they do. Take a man's job away from him and nobody takes anything that he has to say with any seriousness. Writers? Academics? Artists? Ah yes, but in our society the vast majority of people don't consider those people as holding *real* jobs, so they can indulge themselves in whatever they want to say and nobody takes it seriously; in point of fact, nobody even listens. They have come to be considered in our technocratic society as the necessary bric-a-brac of culture, but nobody pays any attention to what they have to say. However, if one of those people should start to work for a daily metropolitan newspaper or a television network, then the vehicle legitimizes their words.

"You would be surprised to discover the number of journalists who have decided it was in their own best interests to stop asking questions or writing 'negative' stories about the RCMP. Not that their decision has been damaging to them. Far from it, in the long run, some of them have gone on to become our leading public personalities.

"How is it done? Well, it is not that everybody responds to the same pressures. But almost everyone has some act they have committed in the past or some interest of theirs that is, shall we say, outside generally accepted behavior, and if brought to light would be damaging, or at least embarrassing. Don't forget that even if you don't have an indiscretion in your closet, it is comparatively easy to dangle some temptation in front of you, or even invent a vice that you have supposedly succumbed to. The variations are endless. And you know, for the reason that I suppose it satisfies certain human needs, it would seem that intelligence organizations have historically been able to attract men and women who were absolutely geniuses in their ability to entrap worthy citizens in scandals not of their own making.

"Oh yes, S understood these diversions of the body and the soul clearly. Why not? He himself was a voluptuary of the flesh. A man who hid that facet of his personality as carefully and as well as he, for so long, must have sought to enjoy his secret and hidden enjoyment, savored by who knows what dark and twisted forms of guilt, with an even deeper gratification than someone who openly wallows in his pleasures.

"No, it certainly wasn't that revelation that led to S's 'early retirement' from the Force. He could have survived that. No, I think in the end it was something else, a much deeper realization, a belated but final awareness on the part of his superiors that S had commitments and motives that went far beyond what they could ever fathom. I think their experience left them unfit to comprehend much more than personal ambition and the symbolic but empty ideals projected by the Force. When you think about it, how could you expect minds like that to ever understand a man as disciplined and as complex as S?

"How did they finally move against him? After Letourneau's abortive surveillance projects had been mercifully brought to an end, he finally began what DV had suggested and what they should have done in the first place: long detailed interrogation. I must say that I have had some experience myself with the art of interrogation, acquired during the war years. I came to appreciate that it was a fine art. I had the privilege of observing several masters of the technique at work. Quiet-spoken, enormously patient men, always solicitous of their charges' health and wellbeing, but who would take the one minute but ambiguous point in the prisoner's story — a point that would have been overlooked by most experienced officers — and work away at it. They were like terriers, mentally shaking and gnawing between their teeth the one flaw in the support. Making the prisoner repeat and mull over the point for hours on end, until the prisoner himself became convinced that he could no longer sustain the illogical weakness of his story. Certainly not in the face of this patient, friendly man, who wanted so much to treat him as an equal, who made the prisoner want to be accepted as an intellectual equal. It is a fascinating process, the art of building a relationship between prisoner and interrogator. Between torturer and tor . . ."

The Old Hand's voice trails off. And the Au. has the feeling that the Old Hand has indulged himself a little too far, that he had not really meant to let that business about torture slip out. He swiftly returns to his central point. "But then with S, the advantage had long been lost. If he had not already become aware of the early

158

surveillance, then those blundering fools who pinned the photograph on his door certainly took any element of surprise out of our hands. He had weeks to prepare himself, mentally and physically for what he knew woud follow: Two weeks of daily interrogation by Letourneau's officers. Ten days by the CIA down in Washington, followed by another two weeks by MI6. And when it was over? Nothing. We are no nearer to knowing whether S is a double agent or not.

The Au. is mystified and stirred by the Old Hand's lapses into the personal, "our hands" and "we are no nearer." Does this mean the Old Hand had been involved in the interrogations? Asked, he brushes aside the Au.'s question with an impatient but graceful wave of his hand, and proceeds with his narrative. "Then you'll never guess what happened? You have to admire the sheer audacity of the man. He sent a letter to the commissioner stating that he had cooperated fully and in good faith with all investigations into his conduct, 'investigations which were a proper and necessary responsibility of a well-organized intelligence service' was the phrase he used, and now he wanted to be cleared and returned to carry out his former duties.

"Well, that threw them into a spin. Letourneau wanted to charge S, 'We have to push him, keep pushing him,' I remember him yelling. But the Commissioner wouldn't have anything to do with it. He had nine months to go before retirement and he didn't want the calm waters of his tenure roiled by the slightest breath of scandal. Nor did any of the other Assistant Commissioners who had done their tour of duty in Security Services prior to Letourneau's arrival. They certainly didn't want anyone rummaging around in their

159

file, to find out why they hadn't demanded more of S. The result was that the Commissioner offered S a transfer to Supply and Services and a position that would put him in charge of the Corps of Commissionaires on the Hill. But S knew exactly where the Commissioner's anxieties would take him. He demanded his old job back or early retirement on full pension. The Commissioner said full pension, only if you get out of the country. He didn't want to leave him around for any inquisitive journalists.

"A week later S was living in retirement on the Channel Islands. I suppose he was quite prepared to spend the rest of his life there until the Solicitor General had him brought back. Why the run for Australia? Yes, that's a good question. That's one I can't understand. His excuse was that he had gone to look up an old uncle who might still be alive. I rather think that, perhaps for the first time in his life, he went into a blue funk. Who knows? Did he think that he wouldn't be able to stand up to another round of interrogations? Had a Soviet defector finally fingered him with evidence that was totally convincing? . . . Who knows?"

A few minutes later the Au. finds himself being courteously ushered out of a side door into a waiting taxi. "It's so much more discreet this way, I'm sure you'll understand," murmurs the Old Hand. And then, just as he is about to get in the cab, the Old Hand detains the Au. with a barely perceptible grip on his elbow. "Did you know that the RCMP Security Services is the only intelligence organization in the world that hasn't had a book written about it? Remarkable, don't you think?"

160

SECTION IX

The city lies uneasy under a leaden sky. Only in the east, where snow threatens, does the sullen grey cloud mass turn to a heavy pink. Dry brown leaves crunch under the shoes of passers-by who hurry themselves through this desolate late autumn scene. The Au. wanders stunned through the sombre streets. Krista is dead. He is still trying to absorb the shock the information has forced on him. Flashes of vivid and uncontrollable imagery leap through his imagination: the heavy, naked man lying in her bed. Krista curled up in the deep leather couch in her sun-filled living room, surrounded by splashes of warm color from the paintings and wall hangings. Police sketches of the "long-haired and knife-wielding youth wanted for . . ." surface as a wild pastiche in his mind's eye.

He had spoken to Krista only the previous afternoon. "Yes, of course," she would be glad to meet him again. She had wondered why he had not called back sooner. When could he come? "Tomorrow afternoon? Perfect." The Au. had been in a quandary. Should he refer to the package of letters and newsclippings, the photograph of Aleayh? He had assumed that she had sent them, but really couldn't be sure. So he refrained from mentioning the envelope and its contents during their telephone conversation. He would follow it up the next day.

But now it was the next day and there was nobody to pursue it with but the ghost of Krista, who invaded his mind in all manner of macabre visions: Krista, alone in the dark, pushing the heavy red and green Flying Pigeon bicycle, ''product of the People's Republic of China,'' feeling nervously in the shadows for the latch to the back gate of her tangled and gloomy garden. The freezing shock at the sudden weight of the hand reaching out of the murk, fumbling for her throat. ''We heard only one scream . . .'' cut short by the long double-sided knife thrusting between *''the anterior sixth and seventh ribs on the left side, puncturing the pericardium, and slicing through the . . .''* The formal language of the pathologist's report could no more stem the flow of jumbled images than could the cool impersonality of the newsstory in the morning newspaper: ''. . . *body of a thirty-five-year-old government interpreter was found just after midnight at the rear of her Fourth Avenue house. Police spokesmen said evidence at the scene indicated the woman had just opened her backyard gate when she was attacked . . . a neighbor reported hearing one short scream.''*

What had she said during that last telephone conversation? ''I wondered why you didn't call sooner.'' What lay behind that statement? Idle politeness, a genuine interest in the Au., or the implication that she had more information about S than she had previously volunteered? The Au. would like to talk to DV. But DV is not available, either at home or at his office.

* * * * *

A weak sun shines fitfully behind the clouds that clutter the sky. Since early morning, light squalls of rain and snow have blustered through the streets. Krista's father, small and silent, a lonely figure in black, his thin white hair blowing erratically in the breeze, watches the funeral director and his assistants carry the coffin to the hearse. Spatters of rain slide over the rich, polished oak wood. A swirling gust of wind blows a newspaper along the sidewalk and wraps it around the leg of one of the pallbearing assistants. He stumbles, then regains his balance. Moving softly, quietly giving directions, the funeral director has everything under control. He opens the back door of the big black Buick and waits for Krista's father and the Au. to enter. Strange that they are the only mourners to attend the funeral of a beautiful and intelligent woman. Where are her friends? (The Au. later learned that the old man had requested a private funeral. "But when you telephoned, I was frankly glad to know you would be there.") The funeral director comes around to the driver's side. He will take them to the cemetery. The hearse and the assistants will follow.

The modest funeral cortege pauses at the high black iron gates of the graveyard. The drizzle shrouds the broad gently sloping hillside in vague wreaths of mist. While the funeral director checks in with the Keeper of the Graves at the cemetery office, a wizened priest under a large black umbrella comes to the car: "Would you like a few words said at the grave?" he asks politely, and then by way of explanation: "I'm retired, officially, but I live in that blue and white house across the street, so I'm keeping up the work. It's only a charge of five dollars." The two old men gaze at each other for a moment: "No, Father, we will have no need of your prayers this morning, thank you," comes the courteous but firm reply. "Well, God bless you then," and the priest returns to the cemetery office.

The funeral director's assistants carry the coffin over strips of brown coconut matting that have been laid over the wet turf. Rain glistens on the black umbrellas. Half in the grave is the grey painted wooden box which will receive the coffin when it is finally lowered into the earth. The pallbearers lay their burden across two rods placed across the open top of the shell. Then they stand back, uncertain. This is not the usual burial. There is no religious ritual laying down forms of behavior. Only the funeral director remains impassive, confident. The Au. is moved to see that the old man is standing at the edge of the grave, tears silently coursing down his seamed cheeks. He stands motionless, head bowed for several long minutes. The rain is coming down harder now. It moves as a curtain in an unfolding skirt-like movement along the cemetery. The assistants shuffle their feet as the dampness begins to creep into the backs of their calves. Finally the old man stoops down for some earth and sprinkles it over the casket. He slowly gestures to the director to do whatever he has to, and then mournfully turns away. The Au. joins him and they walk to the funeral director's car. Behind them they can hear the whine of the motor that lowers the coffin into its grave.

An hour later the Au. sits in the old man's tiny two-room apartment. They are drinking black coffee liberally laced with cognac to "take the chill out of the old bones". They are talking about Spain, the thirties, "Yes, I was there. It's where it all began for most of us. Not too many of the old comrades left now. We used to keep in touch. But you know how it is. If you're not doing specific work for the Party, you tend not to keep up with where everyone is. Although I did write for years to a comrade in Australia. We went through the whole Spanish campaign together. I remember after it was all over, he took me to his home in England. He had a couple of sisters who ran a rooming house at a seaside resort. That's where I first met S. He was just a lad then, about eighteen. He used to sit around and listen wide-eyed to our stories. His uncle made a big impression on him. They were very close. No, I don't know what happened to him. He was in Sydney for a long time, but then he moved away and I lost track of him." The Au. can hardly restrain himself. The questions are about to come pouring out of him, but the old man is suddenly weary. "Thank you for coming to the . . . It's been a lonely time and I appreciate your company. But if you will excuse me, I am feeling terribly tired and have to lie down."

* * * * *

The Old Hand was unrecognizable, drunk beyond coherence and belief. He had not been at the side door to greet the Au. at the appointed hour. But the Au., hearing thuds, shouted exclamations, and aware of the lights blazing at the front of the house, pushed the unlocked door open, and walked down the corridor to the study — former scene of the Old Hand's long patronizing chats. But instead of the calm, smug atmosphere to which the Au. had found himself adapting, a scene of violent chaos: Books, pulled down from their

165

shelves, lay in sprawled and scattered heaps on the floor. Chairs upside down, the upholstery torn out in jagged hunks of cloth. Bottles and glasses in what had been the mirror-lined liquor cabinet, overturned and smashed. In the midst of this disaster, the Old Hand lay slouched in his armchair, all dignity gone from his sweating, fleshy face. His eyes glittering slits behind puffed and swollen flesh. His mouth a red gash, screaming: "THE BASTARD . . . THE LOUSY FUCKING BASTARD! HE BETRAYED US. THE SCUM! US . . . WE WHO HAVE SUPPORTED HIM ALL THESE YEARS. HELD HIM TOGETHER . . ."

The Au. could get no sense out of this sodden middle-aged man lying like a beached whale in the wreckage of his life. He turned to leave. The Old Hand crawled on his hands and knees, cursing: "Just a fuckin' minute there . . ." Rummaged among the piles of books, and randomly ripped some pages from the spine of a volume, then lurched to his feet and stuffed it with mock seriousness into the pocket of the Au.'s corduroy jacket. Then laughing hysterically, he roughly pushed the Au. out the door: "Bugger off, you goddamned hyena," he yelled.

When the Au. had finally found a taxi — not a simple task in the plush enclave of Rockcliffe — he asked the cab driver to turn on the dome light so that he could read the torn pages the Old Hand had stuffed into his coat pocket. He smoothed the crumpled sheets on his knee and discovered the pages covered rules five, six, and seven from the "catechism" of Nachaeyff, the nineteenth century revolutionary:

  5. The revolutionary is a dedicated man, merciless toward the state and altogether merciless

toward the educated classes; and he can expect no mercy from them. Between him and them there exists, declared or concealed, a continual and irreconcilable war ''for life or for death.'' He must accustom himself to enduring torture.

6. Tyrannical toward himself, he must be tyrannical toward others. All the soft and tender affections arising from kinship, friendship, and love, all gratitude and even all honor must be obliterated, and in their place there must be the cold and single-minded passion for the work of revolution. For him there exists only one pleasure, one consolation, one reward, one satisfaction — the success of the revolution. Night and day he must have but one thought, one aim — merciless destruction. Aiming cold-bloodedly and indefatigably toward this end, he must be ready to destroy himself and destroy with his own hands everyone who stands in his way.

7. The nature of the true revolutionary excludes all romanticism, all sensitivity, all exaltations and enthusiasms. He must also exclude private vendettas and personal hatred. The revolutionary passion, practised at every moment of the day until it becomes a habit, is to be employed with cold calculation. At all times and in all places the revolutionary must refuse to allow himself to be guided by his personal impulses, but only by the total submergence of himself in the revolution.

* * * * *

The Lawyer is excited, tense. His voice is guarded and he speaks only in hushed tones: "We can't talk here. We have to get out. C'mon." They walk for a couple of blocks in the rain, then the Lawyer drags the Au. into the National Art Gallery. For a few minutes they walk around the gallery trying to find "a place to talk," but there are too many guards and gallery visitors. The Au. is worried for he believes the Lawyer has been seized by that uncontrollable paranoia that sometimes grips individuals who have spent too much time with representatives from the RCMP SS. The Lawyer finally finds a men's washroom and after carefully checking to see that all the cubicles are empty, perches one hip on a tiled sink and begins:

"The inquiry is closed. It's all over. Wait a minute . . . (a hand raised, demanding patience.) S is gone. Yeah, that's right. No, I mean yes, he made a deal, or rather *they* made a deal with the Solicitor General. Listen! Let me give it to you from the top. This morning S took me aside. He told me very coldly and precisely that he was fed up with all this horseshit. He asked me to call over this bird who has been sitting as an 'observer' in the inquiry since it began. I always wondered who he was. Turned out he is the RCMP liaison officer to the CIA in Washington. 'Okay, Brandy,' said S. 'Get in touch with Letourneau. I know he's hanging around and tell him to get hold of the SG. Tell them that tomorrow morning I'm going to start talking about Operation Featherbed. Now get moving. Because I need a couple of hours with my lawyer.' Brandy gave him a hard icy look. Not, I think, because he didn't like being talked to in that manner, but kind of 'now your days are numbered' stare, and left in a hurry.

"It didn't take S two hours to tell me about Operation Featherbed. In fact, it took less than half an hour, but even now, six hours later, I'm still pondering the implications of what he told me. Briefly then: It seems that Letourneau, at the same time he ordered the electronic surveillance of S's house, also started the investigation Operation Featherbed. It began on the premises that if S was a double agent, then he would have to have had a fairly high-level support group to sustain him all these years.

"There were four investigators assigned. DV was one, and so was this guy Brandy. They started way back, 1948, before S even arrived on the scene. They went into the archives and opened up all the files and evidence that Mackenzie King had ordered sealed because he had been afraid of a witch hunt in the civil service. They carefully examined all the material that surrounded the Gouzenko investigations. Then they studied the 1947 Taschereau hearings, which were held in camera, and took evidence from every single individual no matter how peripherally involved in the Gouzenko investigations. It seems that under the Official Secrets Act, the Taschereau files have been sealed for more than twenty-five years.

"After several months of poring over this mass of files and documents, the investigation team put together a group of names. And you know what? It turned out that this group was the central core of S's famous trapline: all the guys who over the years had made their way up through the ranks of the civil service to heads of departments and crown corporations, assistant deputy ministers and even two deputy ministers. For the last fifteen years, these are the people he met with, either singly or in pairs, for a quiet dinner or

169

a drink after work in the evening. All of these people had sensitive jobs in terms of the political and economic information they handled on a daily basis for their departments. Sure, budgets, defense procurement programs, and I understand in a couple of cases access to secret information on the development of military technology in the United States. Right, exactly . . . . all 'the meat and potatoes' of a foreign intelligence-gathering service. You've got the picture.

"That's it, you're away ahead of me. This presents two questions: First, what did Letourneau do with the results from Operation Featherbed? Only Letourneau can answer that one, but let's suppose that he did what he should have done, what his job demanded: That he went to the Prime Minister with the information that suggested his federal civil service had been infiltrated at its highest levels by agents of a foreign intelligence service. And then, say the Prime Minister — who for reasons for which we have no inkling —·refused to accept or act on this information. What would you do if you were the Director General of Intelligence? You would resign, wouldn't you? And isn't that exactly what Letourneau did four years ago?

"Okay, let's go to the second question: How come S knew all about this investigation? After all, it was supposed to be a secret operation directed at him and at his support group. And there is no doubt from the deal that was made, that it came as a complete shock to the RCMP that he knew all about Operation Featherbed. Naturally I asked him how he found out about the investigation. At first he wouldn't answer the question. Then when I pressed the point, he just said: 'I wouldn't be much of a counter-espionage officer if I didn't realize when I was the target of an investigation,' and I had to leave it at that.

"But then when Inspector Brandy came back, he had a very pale Solicitor General in tow. The SG had the kind of 'Oh, my God, what did I start?' kind of expression. The meeting didn't take long. It was obvious that it had all been worked out in the PM's office. The SG said that "for reasons that have to do with the security of the state the inquiry has been terminated." His office would prepare an airline ticket to return S to Australia or his home in the Channel Islands, whatever he wanted. His office was also preparing a generous cheque to compensate S for his time and inconvenience. And yes, his legal expenses — meaning me — were taken care of. He shook S's hand with a brief limp-rag gesture and then he left. S offered his hand to Inspector Brandy who lingered for a moment. But Brandy wouldn't shake hands. He had the face of a man who thought he had stepped into an elevator but instead found himself tumbling headlong down the empty shaft. Although he did manage to get off a cryptic, 'I guess I'll be seeing you around Washington, then,' more as a statement than a question.

"Frankly, my head was spinning. As I said, I'm still trying to work out the implications of it all. But just before he left, I did ask S why he had been so confident that he would get his deal. His answer? The PM is going into an election this year. He could never risk the information on Operation Featherbed being presented to the three members of parliament. It would be impossible for him to survive such an enormous scandal. So he had to cover it up by stopping the inquiry.

EPILOGUE

The winter over, the Au. heard that DV had left the
Force and, according to reports he received, "had
fallen to serious drinking." Through the spring and
summer DV made his headquarters at the pub below
the National Arts Centre. He "seemed to take a strange
delight in taking on the yahoos who frequent the pub
late in the evening." Apparently these troublemakers
would become incensed at the solitude in which DV
wrapped himself. For even though he drank "slowly
and steadily through the evening, he was always reading a book or magazine."

After he had thrown three or four of them into the
canal, they apparently learned to leave him in peace —
"He did it with such ease. Once the waiter tried to
steer a troublemaker away from DV's table. But DV
said, very politely, mind you, 'No, let me take care of
it,' and splash! no scuffle, no blows exchanged, the
jerk went flying through the air and into the canal."

The Au. is inclined to believe that gossip tended to
exaggerate DV's supposed alcoholic intake. There
were too many years of physical discipline in the
man's background. And because other reports still had
him out at seven every morning for his daily run along
the canal towpath.

The Au. had left Ottawa to live in Toronto even before the winter set in, and had written several letters to DV, but none of them were answered. Then the Au. left the country for several months and, when he came back, found that DV had left Ottawa without leaving a forwarding address. But in January, during the winter of '76/77, the Au. — once again living in Toronto — took his eight-year-old son to a downtown ice-hockey rink for a practice with his teammates.

The Au. settled down on a bench in the empty stands to enjoy the Sunday morning ritual. He delighted in the children's enthusiastic shouts, the cold hard smell of the ice, the bright sweaters, and the echoing boom of pucks bouncing off the boards. Then he caught sight of a familiar heavy-set man, quietly but enthusiastically coaching a squad of boys through a practice session at the other end of the rink. The Au. waited until the session was over before joining DV. He was not altogether surprised that DV was cool and uninterested. Yes, he was the manager of the rink now, and was enjoying life, "Should have done this years ago." He declined an invitation for a Chinese dinner or a drink to talk things over, "There's nothing I want to talk about. For me, that's all over." And then, with a brusque, "Excuse me, I have another bunch of boys to take care of," he turned his back on the Au.

* * * * *

That spring the Au. was invited to dine at the EA's favorite health food restaurant in Toronto. The Executive Assistant had resigned from his job with the Solicitor General's office and was on his way to England:

"Travel for the summer through Europe, then Lon-

173

don School of Economics for a year or two. Why not? It's the same route the PM took.'' And even as he finished chuckling. ''Listen, I thought you might like to know. S is working down in Latin America. Yeah, I guess retirement was too quiet for him. He works for a CIA-front organization that operates out of one of those multinationals that are taking over the economy down there. How long do I think he was working for the CIA? How can you ever figure it out? Perhaps they even had him turned around since 1964 when the Nosenko defection fingered S as a KGB agent. Quite a pivotal position, wouldn't you say? Once the CIA had S turned around they could use him to extract all the important Canadian stuff for themselves and then, through him, pump any crap they wanted along to the Soviets.

''Krista Gollner? It seems that she was a KGB agent who attempted to penetrate the CIA by going to work for them. Unlike S, she retained her original loyalties. Did S turn her in? Perhaps, again, who knows?

''Yeah, I guess you can say that S won — if you call that winning. I dunno, where else is there to go, when as a triple-agent you have blown two-thirds of your act? Yes, as a matter of fact, I checked. He still gets his RCMP pension check.

''The Taschereau Papers? Some military intelligence type in the PM's office has spent the last year laundering the documents: destroying evidence, erasing names; generally rewriting history under the protection of our security laws.

''I wouldn't worry too much about the SS. They seem to have adapted to the shock of it all quite well. Why not? After all, the United States manipulates every other area of our lives, we shouldn't have too much trouble accommodating ourselves to the fact that the CIA manipulated our intelligence services all these years, and from the top at that. So what? It's all part of being a colony."

Ian Adams,
July, 1977.
Toronto.

ROUTES TO THE TOP OF RCMP SECURITY SERVICES

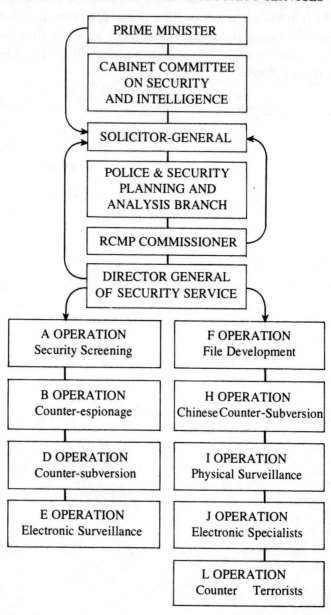

PRIME MINISTER

CABINET COMMITTEE
ON SECURITY
AND INTELLIGENCE

SOLICITOR-GENERAL

POLICE & SECURITY
PLANNING AND
ANALYSIS BRANCH

RCMP COMMISSIONER

DIRECTOR GENERAL
OF SECURITY SERVICE

A OPERATION
Security Screening

F OPERATION
File Development

B OPERATION
Counter-espionage

H OPERATION
Chinese Counter-Subversion

D OPERATION
Counter-subversion

I OPERATION
Physical Surveillance

E OPERATION
Electronic Surveillance

J OPERATION
Electronic Specialists

L OPERATION
Counter   Terrorists